FA... ...TTERS

PROSE SERIES 60

Canadä

Guernica Editions Inc. acknowledges support of
The Canada Council for the Arts.
Guernica Editions Inc. acknowledges support from the Ontario Arts Council.
Guernica Editions Inc. acknowledges the financial support of the
Government of Canada through the Book Publishing Industry Development
Program (BPIDP).

MARISA DE FRANCESCHI

FAMILY MATTERS

*For Gil,
a sample of
my work.
Hope you like it.
Marisa De Franceschi*

GUERNICA
TORONTO·BUFFALO·LANCASTER (U.K.)
2001

Antonio D'Alfonso, editor
Guernica Editions Inc.
P.O. Box 117, Station P, Toronto (ON), Canada M5S 2S6
2250 Military Road, Tonawanda, N.Y. 14150-6000 U.S.A.
Gazelle, Falcon House, Queen Square, Lancaster LA1 1RN U.K.

Printed in Canada.
First edition.

Legal Deposit – First Quarter
National Library of Canada
Library of Congress Catalog Card Number: 2001095235
De Franceschi, Marisa
Family matters
(Prose series ; 60)
ISBN 1-55071-141-5
I. Title.
PS8557.E36F34   2001 C813'.54   C2001-902475-4
PR9199.3.D355.F34 2001

(.Ʞ.U) я

CONTENTS

ACKNOWLEDGMENTS

Earlier versions of some of these stories appeared in the following publications: "Peonies Trying to Survive" in the anthology, *Ricordi:Things Remembered*, Guernica Editions, 1989, "Royal Blood" was the recipient of The Okanagan Short Story Award and published in the magazine, *Canadian Author & Bookman*, 1984, and was included in the anthology, *Pure Fiction*, Fitzhenry & Whiteside, 1986, "The Providers" was the recipient of The Okanagan Short Story Award and published in the magazine, *Canadian Author & Bookman*, 1980, and was included in the anthology, *Pure Fiction*, Fitzhenry & Whiteside, 1986, "Things Remembered" in the anthology *Investigating Women*, Simon & Pierre, 1995, "The T-Shirt Man" in *The Toronto Review of Contemporary Writing Abroad*, 1995.

My father's name was John and my first serious boyfriend's name was John too. But that, according to my Dad, was the only thing John, the boyfriend, had going for him.

John, the boyfriend, was a pretty ordinary looking fellow. He had carrot red hair my mother abhorred due to the fact that many of the relatives on her side of the family were carrot tops, with the added misfortune of being rather dim-witted. Thus, in her mind, hair coloring and intelligence correlated. She herself was a brunette and sharp as a tack.

Long before I ever met John, I remember her always telling me how petrified she was when she'd discovered she was going to have a baby. "I was so afraid I'd have a redhead," she used to say. "I don't know what I would have done if you'd been born with red hair, Marlena."

Those words always sent shivers up my spine. I couldn't help thinking I'd been saved from some sort of horrid fate thanks to the luck of a gene that gave me proper, chestnut-colored hair. What would she have done had I come up with the short end of the stick, I used to wonder? Give me up for adoption? Abandon me in the forest where she claimed she'd found me? The possibilities gave me goose bumps.

John, the boyfriend, made matters worse by sporting a crew cut, which was the style then. Even I have to admit, it did little for him. All he had to do was look at himself in the mirror and it would have told him his square face was made more square by the sheered, flat top. Not to mention how this North American aberration was in sharp contrast to my father and uncles' dark, wavy locks sensually framing their Mediterranean faces. They had the sort of hair immortalized by the Renaissance sculptors, like the marble curls of Michelangelo's David. But John wouldn't have been one to primp and preen like these other men who were always standing at the mirror in adoration of their fine features. Meticulous in their grooming, they were forever trimming their mustaches just so. Snip, snip, as precise as surgeons. I'd watch them squeeze a dab of hair cream into the palm of a hand, rub it about, then, with arms held high over their heads and great sweeping motions, they ran it through their tresses as they combed and patted their locks into place.

John had beady little eyes that seemed to squint all the time and his lashes were a faint shade of reddish-blond and barely visible. His complexion was just a mass of freckles. I had never seen anyone with as many freckles as John. They had taken complete possession of his face and looked like insect bites on the mend. No swarthy skin for him.

He was short and compact, and I could never wear heels because I'd tower over him being so tall myself. And he did have bowed legs. My father said, when you saw him from behind, it looked as if he'd been on a horse too long and he'd been molded into the saddle. My mother said he kind of reminded her of a bulldog. She admitted he looked sturdy and tough, but a Cocker Spaniel he was not.

Sure, I wasn't blind. I could see John was not the best looking guy in the world. But somehow he grew on you. Seeing him at school, day after day, he seemed to get less and less unattractive and, as time went on, he wasn't ugly at all. On the contrary, when he occasionally beamed that smile of his, my heart went out to him.

He was a fine and dedicated athlete on all the school

teams and played his fair share of the basketball and football games which I diligently attended as the official girlfriend.

But, as far as my family was concerned, none of his attributes made up for the fact that he was not attractive.

The first time he came to the house, my little sister went to let him in. I remember him standing in the doorway silhouetted by the daylight behind him and me cringing at the sight of all that light coming through his bowed legs, afraid my father would notice. My little sister was aghast and, when she walked into the kitchen to tell my mother John was waiting for me, I heard her say, "Poor Marlena."

No, he was not tall, dark and handsome like my father and his brothers, uncle Tony and uncle Joe who liked to brag how they were always being mistaken for Clark Gable, Carey Grant, or Rock Hudson: silver screen idols of the time. Dad was Gable incarnate, mustache and all, and he loved to tell how, on his first transatlantic trip back home on the ocean liner, S.S. France, women swarmed around him convinced he was indeed the actor. Uncle Joe was the Carey Grant look-alike and uncle Tony was Rock Hudson. Years later, when we all learned Hudson's secret, there was no end to the snickering and teasing at poor uncle Tony's expense. Virility and masculinity, done up in a handsome body, were top priorities for these men.

But I was just happy to have a boy call on me. I wasn't going to be fussy. After all, I was no walking poster girl of female pulchritude myself. What did I expect? That someone like Roy Thompson: wealthy, handsome, blond and a top notch swimmer would ever look at the likes of me? Although John was actually Scottish, and thus a Brit, he seemed foreign like me. Most of the time he had that pained, grieving look on his face, that lack of confidence, that "I'm not sure what the hell I'm supposed to be doing" expression that I myself had.

I blamed his hapless lack of confidence on the fact that he had no mother. She had died several years before when John was but a child and he'd been left with an older sister, who did the best she could, and a father who seemed like the most joyless man on the face of the earth. The father ran a corner store before the days of Seven-11's and such. The store was near the school and, on our way home, we kids used to stop in for gum drops, jelly beans, or jaw breakers. He sold them two or three at a time, if that was what you asked for, and I remember him going patiently from candy bin to candy bin plucking out two of these and three of those as we pointed to the sweet, tooth decaying treats. They weren't wrapped in those days and now I wince at the thought of him touching all the candies which would end up in our mouths. Every time he went to the candy counter and slid open the glass door, he leaned on it as if he needed it for support. I don't recall him ever smiling or talking to us. He just mechanically told us what we owed him, collected the change and dropped it into the till, then slumped back down over the counter as if the transaction had depleted him of all his energy.

When my father asked what John's father did for a living, I said he owned some sort of store and was a *businessman*.

"Hrump," my father said. And nothing more. I knew the word *businessman* would shut him up.

My white lie about John's father mattered little to me. If that was what it took to keep my parents quiet, I was quite willing to commit the venial sin. I could always have it cleaned off my slate by telling the priest at confession.

My father was a heavy equipment mechanic. He was

pretty proud of that. Unlike most of his Italian immigrant friends, he didn't dig ditches or mix cement by hand in a wheelbarrow but rather worked for a large builders supply company that manufactured a variety of concrete products. They also had a large fleet of ready mixers that could hold several cubic meters of cement which was kept turning to keep it from settling while en route to job sites to pour concrete footings, driveways, sidewalks and any number of construction projects. His job was to keep these elephantine machines running smoothly as well as making sure the plant itself operated without a glitch.

In spite of all the wisecracks and put-downs, I think my parents had decided not to be overly critical, since finally someone had taken interest in their eldest daughter.

I think my mother was probably most relieved. I'd seen the disappointment on her face many a time. Whenever she combed my hair and attempted to fashion different styles, then gave up and just parted it on the left swinging the rest to the right and fastening it with a bobby pin, she looked frustrated. I hated that style and she never knew the minute I was out of her sight, I pulled that bobby pin out, hid it in my pocket and let the hair fall all over my face. If I was as ugly as they made me feel, I was going to conceal as much of myself as possible.

There were all sorts of ways she conveyed to me the idea that I was no Venus de Milo. She didn't have to actually say it, although plenty of my other relatives had no qualms about routinely telling me I was so pathetically thin I looked anorexic. Because of my legs, I was nicknamed "celery sticks" by my uncle Joe. My uncle Tony, who was really good at stripping me of self confidence, would say things like, "Hey, Marlena, can I borrow one of your toothpicks?," meaning my legs. As if this thinness wasn't enough of a curse, my legs were also as hairy as any man's. Whenever uncle Tony rinsed out wine bottles he'd shout, "Marlena, can I borrow your bottle brushes?"

"You take after your father's side of the family," my mother would pronounce, meaning I was hairy like them. A good thing if you were male; not so good if you were me.

"She doesn't take after you," my uncles would chorus.

She wouldn't allow me to shave insisting I was too young and, besides, shaving would make the hair grow back thicker and darker, she claimed. At school, everybody made fun of me. If they didn't actually say things out loud, their stares and snickers spoke for them. I wore knee socks even in summer.

When I started to sprout breasts and it looked as if I had a couple of hard peas under my shirt, uncle Tony would come over and tweak my nipples and say, "Look, everybody, Marlena's got little tits." No amount of crying stopped the torment. In fact, it made matters worse. My mother would tell me I was too sensitive for my own good. "Stop being such a ninny," she'd yell. "They're only teasing." I wanted to say, but they don't tease you.

I can't for the life of me understand how they could have been so cruel to a young child. They all seemed to lack any kind of sensitivity. They were perverse in their desire to degrade and make fun of you if you didn't live up to their standards. They had only one template to fit you to: theirs. There was a meanness of spirit in them I could never comprehend. It was as if they deliberately set out to destroy you, to wound you, as if all this bantering was a fencing match to see who drew blood first. Like heat sensing missiles, they would target your weaknesses and vulnerabilities and home in with devastating accuracy. Then, once they'd hit the bull's eye, they'd laugh and say, "We're only joking."

How I prayed my uncles would marry and move out. But women over here weren't interested in these dark creatures with the wife beater undershirts. All these men could hope for was some immigrant woman, and there weren't many of those around then. They had to be imported, which is what happened eventually, but not soon enough for me.

Some good came of all this. I learned how not to behave with my own child, whom I named Johnny, and gave him enough confidence for a tribe. Funny how my father always took it for granted my son was his namesake. He never realized I'd named him after John, the boyfriend.

In my mother's defense, she at least tried to be diplomatic. I have to think now how young she was herself back then and how ignorant she must have been about child rearing and the different stages a child goes through. Although she did seem to know about "the ugly stage." When I was ten or eleven she always used to try to make me feel better by saying, "You'll grow out of it. It's just the ugly stage."

I have to remind myself she'd spent the better part of her youth trying to survive a war in Europe. The do's and don't's of how to raise children could not have been a priority. She wasn't one to read up on such things. Besides, the market wouldn't have been saturated with all the child care and self help stuff we have today. Then, too, when she got to America she wouldn't have been able to read since she didn't know English.

I was burdened with the added misfortune that she herself was a stunning beauty. The Sofia Loren type. In her mid-twenties, and as ripe as an autumn peach, she was a man's woman, rounded out in all the right places. She had large, expressive breasts which seemed even bigger because of her tiny waist. My Dad proudly showed us how he could circle her waist with his two hands. Then she bloomed out with the greatest set of hips this side of the Atlantic.

Whenever I walked with her, I saw men turn their heads and stare, heard car horns honk, whistles and all sorts of gritty remarks I didn't always understand. How I wished they did that to me. She had the most beautiful set of legs, as perfect as my doll's. Dad always told the story about the first time he saw those legs walking up the church steps in our home town and how he told his brothers, then and there, he was going to "reel that one in." How would I ever survive with my celery sticks?

I remember once, she took me to the finest shoe store in the city. I guess she'd convinced herself that if she bought me expensive shoes, somehow they would make my skinny legs look less thin. Saddle oxfords were in vogue then and she was always one to follow the latest trends. But the bulky brown and white leather footwear accentuated my scrawny calves. As I paraded in front of her modeling the shoes, she just sobbed and sobbed, and I wished the ground beneath my feet would just swallow me up and take me out of her sight.

I would ask her, "Mom, will I have legs like yours one day?"

She'd always say, "Of course you will."

"When?" I'd pester.

"When you turn fourteen," she'd say.

I remember being naive enough at that age to honestly believe the night before my fourteenth birthday that I would wake up the next morning with legs like hers. Of course, that never happened.

With John I felt prettier than I'd ever felt before. There was something about the way he looked at me from across the classroom. He was the first man to make me feel beautiful even if I didn't look like my mother.

I thought John was brave too. Brave to go out with a girl like me with skinny, hairy legs and no breasts. A foreigner at that. I wasn't stupid. I'd heard him being teased about the greasy Dago. I had no idea of the literal meaning of the word but I knew it wasn't a nice thing to be called.

On the night that was to leave an indelible mark on me, I had gone to the football game to watch John win for our school. It was all-city championships and John was the hero. He'd scored the winning touchdown and I'd been there to witness the miracle.

I remember the crowd springing up from bleachers in ecstacy and the football team hoisted John up on their shoulders and everyone chanted his name. What a moment that must have been for him.

A dance followed in the evening in the school gym and everyone was coming by to congratulate John and, for once in his short life, he beamed with pride.

The big tough guys on the team came by and slapped him hard on the back and said things like, "Way to go, John," and "We knew you had it in you," and "Gonna score with the Dago tonight?"

I guess all the attention and such boosted his self confidence because that night, as we walked home, he held my hand and then on my front porch he sort of embraced me and pulled my body up close to his. I was wearing flats and was just about level with him and I could feel a squirming but steady stiffness down near my private parts.

Sure, I had heard all about boys and their penises and how they were forever trying to stick them in you, but I'd never personally come anywhere near such an occurrence. I was convinced nice people like myself and John didn't do such grotesque things.

I'd never been this close to a boy before. The smell of his school leather jacket seared my nostrils. I could hear his breathing now and it startled me. I'd never heard anyone breathe that way. Almost like my dog panting or maybe it was like the way you breathe after running a good distance or playing hard.

He planted a dry kiss on my parched lips and it surprised me because it just sort of tickled. It certainly didn't give me any sensual pleasure. It was like kissing my ceramic doll, not at all like touching real, live flesh. It was obvious neither of us knew much about kissing then. But I have to give John an "A" for effort. He just stuck his closed lips against my equally closed lips and pressed. We just pressed and pressed and pressed as if we were trying to squeeze some pleasure out of this activity. We'd both seen actors doing this in the movies and they seemed to be enjoying it.

It was during this pressing that the porch light went on, startling us out of our wits. I looked up and saw my father's face in the doorway and nearly disintegrated in shame. My father's dark eyes were as large as saucers and they were filled with rage and fury. I could see his jaw tightening and I knew he was ready to explode.

Stupid, stupid, I said to myself. How could I be so stupid? To do such a thing on our front porch. To have ruined my life, because I knew, then and there, my father would never let me forget it, to have ruined my life for this – whatever it was – this kiss, this pressing of the lips.

John let go of me like the proverbial hot potato and his squinty eyes opened wide. He didn't say anything. Nothing at all. He simply let go of me and dashed off the front porch like a rabbit caught in headlights and raced down the street.

For the longest time, I couldn't look my father in the eye after that. Every time I tried, the image of me and John pressing our cold, dry lips together came up and a flush of embarrassment raced through my body. Even now that I'm old, the memory shoots adrenalin through me, and I feel stupid.

John and I didn't see much of each other after that. I don't know if it was because my father caught us kissing or if it was because our experiment in sexuality had been such a flop, but we went our separate ways. By the end of that year, I had enrolled at the local university while he planned to become a fireman.

The last week of June there was going to be a class party at a local beach with a dance pavilion. I hadn't even bothered to ask if I could go. I had no desire to be a wallflower.

"Walking home?" John asked, as he came up to my locker.

I nodded yes.

"Can I walk with you?" he asked.

"Sure," I replied.

As we approached the place where we parted, he stopped and asked hesitantly, "Going to the dance tonight?"

I nodded yes. "I'm on cash," I told him. "As soon as Sherry relieves me I'll be in the gym." That had been the only way I managed to go to the dance: join the dance committee and lie to my parents it was a "school thing" I had to do.

"See you then," he said.

We communicated with blushes, sweaty hands and brows, racing hearts and meaningful gestures like John carrying my books home or me waiting for him after football practice.

A rumbling in the western sky made me quicken my pace. "Looks like rain," I said. Menacing clouds were building at an urgent pace, the grey formations piling up on each other as a prelude for the fury to come. I recognized the threat since we lived in what everyone called Tornado Alley, a place where there was always a chance a twister would touch down and often did. The rumbling intensified, and I felt the first tentative drops of rain. "Hurry," I said, "Or we'll get wet."

But John didn't hurry. Instead he said, "I love storms. Love the sound of them. Especially the sound of the rain pelting my window or dancing on the roof. I could listen to that for hours."

I just looked at him, amazed he would tell me such an intimate thing. "Rain . . . dancing on the roof." I remember thinking, this is what I liked about John. This gentleness.

Ever since then, rain makes me think of John. Even now, so many years later.

He stopped and said, "Listen. Can you go to the class beach party with me?"

I didn't know what to say. Again I thought he was pretty brave to be asking me after that incident with my father.

"I'll let you know," I told him. I started for home. He ran after me. "Marlena," he called. "Wait." He took off his leather jacket and tossed it over my shoulders. When I looked back at John, he was just sauntering along as if the sky hadn't opened up to deliver torrents of rain, as if the flashes of lightning weren't ominous.

My parents said I could go, probably relieved someone had asked me. But I had to be home by nine in the evening. There was no discussing the matter. No compromising. Reminding them it was still daylight at that time didn't help.

My father said, "Precisely," and I knew what he was think-ing.

John said that would be fine. He'd ask Ted, a friend of his who had a car, to get me home before my curfew.

But, of course, when the time came, Ted and his girl-friend, Angie, didn't want to leave. John begged, "Look, Ted, you promised. Her parents'll skin her alive. Come on. You promised."

The fear of being late welled up in me and I began to feel sick. John could tell I was getting pretty upset. He went over to Ted and pleaded, "Ted, I'll pay for the whole tank of gas. Just let's get her home."

Ted and Angie glared at me with such scorn. The bribe worked, however, and they got up from their beach towels, shook them out and moved towards the car. I heard Ted mutter, "Damned stupid Dagos."

We hadn't driven more than five minutes when I asked Ted to stop the car. I was going to be sick.

"Just hold it in till you get home," he said, as if this was something I could control.

But that was impossible and so I vomited all over the back seat. He screeched to a stop.

"What the hell?" he roared.

"Gross," Angie said scrunching up her face and covering her nose and mouth with her hands.

"She told you to pull over," John said protectively.

I threw up twice more before we got home. Only those times Ted did pull over when I told him to.

My parents were on the front porch like stone sentinels. Ted didn't bother to pull in the driveway. He just dropped me off curbside like a bag of garbage.

I remember running up to the infamous porch where my

mother greeted me with a powerful slap across my face. I can't for the life of me remember what happened next. They must have yelled at me and I probably went to my room to cry. But I can't recall. I was so embarrassed because I was sure John and Ted and Angie had seen it all.

The last time I saw John, he was at a local Mall doing some fire prevention thing. I stopped to say hello. I was pregnant, and I remember him looking at my big belly and I wanted to tell him I'd come a long way since that pressing of the lips. I'd learned one had to part them, for one thing, and let the tongues explore one another. But I didn't say anything of the kind. I just asked politely how he was doing and he did the same with me. I remember him looking at me the way he did when we were in high school and again he made me feel beautiful, despite the fact I was all puffed up and my belly looked like one of my father's ready mixers.

The next morning, when the clock radio flicked on with the six o'clock news I heard about a local fireman, John Smith, who had had a fatal accident during the night. At first I was sure John had been called to a blazing building and had died in it. But it wasn't a fire at all. A car accident. He'd been driving down the highway late at night and struck a concrete pillar at an overpass. The jaws of life had to be used to extricate his mangled body from the scrunched up wreck.

There was a picture of him in the local paper. It was one of those taken the night he scored the winning touchdown. The night my father caught us on the porch.

I knew my parents would see it. When they came over for coffee that night, my mother said, "Isn't that the ugly redhead you used to go out with in high school?"

My face turned crimson both from embarrassment and

anger. I knew what my father was thinking and I hated my mother for calling John "the ugly redhead." I wanted to throw the paper at them. Tell them John wasn't an ugly redhead, but a kind and sensitive man who loved listening to the rain dancing on the roof.

TOMATO SEASON

Tomato season plunged into full swing by mid-August. That was when my mother, in addition to already working seven days at the canning factory she managed out in the county, added on the night shift. Our home life became hectic with her leaving early each morning, well before my father got up for work. I, in my turn, took one of the company buses to the plant. Although our destinations were the same, I didn't ride in the car with her because she needed to be down there early to make sure all was "ship shape" before the workers arrived. The buses took much longer to get to the factory since they had to make several stops to pick up the "peelers," the women who worked for my mother. And also, my mother liked me on the bus for practical reasons. It gave me a chance to see how the driver was behaving and what mood the women were in and I could report all this back to her. I felt like a spy.

When the night shift was tacked on, my mother would leave the factory early to go home for a short nap and to throw together some semblance of dinner for my Dad before driving back out again. So, when the plant ran practically round the clock like this, I had no choice but to take the bus home.

I hated that early morning drive with all those smelly, dark-haired women my mother hired, year after year, to peel tomatoes, and I hated the drive home at night even more when the stench of sweat and tomatoes and dirty, oily, unwashed hair was so intense I would gag if I didn't hold my hand over my nose and mouth. But that was tomato season for you. You got up at four in the morning, took one of the buses for the hour and a half ride to the factory, worked ten hours, then lifted your weary carcass back on the bus and the ride home, exhausted. A few weeks of that made everybody cranky and it was all they could do to get enough sleep, never mind primping and preening. Except for a few summer students like myself, all these women had families and husbands to take care of. They didn't stop cooking and doing the wash just because they had their summer jobs. On the contrary, the kinds of husbands most of these women had would say something like, "Go ahead. Go to work if you want. Just don't use that as an excuse to let things go at home . . . as long as my dinner's on the table . . . " Women's lib was not an issue in those days for those people.

These schizophrenic men wanted "the chicken and the egg," my mother used to say. In order not to loose face, they had to put on an act, pretend they, as breadwinners and providers, were insulted by their women working but all the while they carefully counted the dollars their handmaids brought in on payday.

These women, I must admit however, were as hungry for money as wolves for fresh kill, much like their mates. They all longed for the day they could go back to Italy on vacation laden like beasts of burden with gifts to impress the relatives never letting on that the nitty gritty of their lives was filled with drudgery and hardship.

If the women played their cards right and peeled enough tomatoes, they could bring home cheques as fat as their husbands' who mostly worked on construction. If my mother played her cards right she could make in a few months as much as my Dad did all year, although my Dad never acknowledged this little ripple in their lives preferring,

I suppose, to accept the fruits of her labour as one gladly accepts a windfall. He was never one to enjoy the taste of his own sweat. I'm certain that, deep down, his thoughts on my mother's job gravitated instinctively towards the feelings these other men verbalized. But he chose to ignore it all, which was both good and bad, allowing my mother a taste of freedom but giving her no recognition. Oh, it was true he and my mother were by then well past the stage her peelers were at, having been in this country for years. Her women and their families were still firmly shackled to the old ways. To some extent, she was too. But my mother drove a car, spoke the language well, and could even read and write enough of it to make do. She'd rightfully earned some sense of emancipation by then, though she was still careful to give him no cause for complaint.

The reason these summer jobs could be so lucrative was because it was "piece work." County tomato growers hauled their harvest to the plant where they dumped their precious plump fruit on to conveyor belts to be jet washed and scalded with hot water to loosen the skins. From there the tomatoes jiggled and wiggled and danced like models on a runway on their way to other belts where the dark women stood waiting to grab and peel and plop them into shiny tin cans, counting all the while and keeping track of their earning in their heads. For these women, all those steamed and scalded tomatoes were copper pennies. The more you peeled, the more money you made, and when the "punchers" came by – which is what I was most of the time – they counted the cans and punched a hole for every dozen into a stiff card that hung in front of each peeler. At the end of the day, my mother collected all the cards, counted the dozens and at the end of the week, she added it all up and the women were paid accordingly and she was paid a percentage of that. It was to everyone's advantage to work hard and fast, and take little if any time off. If you didn't want to stop for lunch, that was your prerogative. The belts ran continuously.

This seemed to me the essence of the self-reliant worker, the employee who unquestionably earned every cent by the sweat of her brow. No frills and perks here, no benefit packages and paid holidays and dental plans. No unions to bargain for you. It was every woman for herself.

But this did cause certain problems. Some of the peelers wouldn't take time off to tape a cut finger and even though the acid in the tomatoes stung their cuts, they allowed them to bleed and the blood would run into the cans. No one could tell because it was all the same colour.

Although the prospect of earning some money was an incentive for me too, it was not my primary one. I put up with the drudgery because of Tom Dresser, the boss's son. I had such a crush on him I probably would have walked across burning coals if that was the price I had to pay for his company. Getting up at four in the morning and riding the buses was well worth the rewards I'd reap.

Tom was a summer student like me. Only a bit older. He attended some prestigious university in Kingston, while I was still in high school. We'd both worked at his father's factory before, but this summer I must have changed a lot because he actually started to pay attention to me.

Just before arriving at the plant, I would adjust my makeup and check in my mirror that my hairnet, an unattractive but obligatory item, didn't flatten my hair too much. I would jut out my sprouting breasts and I wouldn't tie on my ugly plastic apron till the last minute.

My mother always had a cup of hot coffee and a doughnut ready for me when I got to the factory. She and I took a few minutes together once the belts began rolling with red tomatoes and with the shiny cans which clanked their hollow wind-chime twang as they paraded down the chute on the way to their own conveyor belts which ran parallel to the wide ones the tomatoes rode on. In order to get these few minutes she'd had to implement a schedule for the peelers, who were always fighting like schoolchildren to get to the front of the line to claim their places, vying for the best spots where they could grab the biggest tomatoes to fill their cans faster. She'd devised a system whereby the first three women on the line went to the end the following day and the next three moved up. The factory floor was a bit more civilized once these measures were put in place. Grudgingly, like reprimanded children, they accepted the new order, although there were still squabbles when a woman stretched a greedy hand ahead to snatch what theoretically wasn't hers.

Since I wouldn't have to start punching until some of the women had canned their first dozens, we could sip our coffee and talk.

The sight of my mother thrilled me every time I arrived at the plant and saw her with Mr. Dresser, the boss and Tom's father, standing by the main entrance to greet all the women who filed in like cattle. She was so unlike the peelers. They were frumpy and unkempt in their dark, uncoordinated clothes while she was the picture of composure in her white uniform, always spotless at the beginning of each shift. She had a closet full of these uniforms and could afford to change as often as she wished. Neat and trim, like a well pruned rose, she basked in the attention her position afforded her. She'd welcome the women with a smile and encouraging words and comments on their welfare, speaking in Italian: "Yolanda, did you sleep well last night?" "Stella, is the baby feeling better?" "Maria, how's that finger? . . . Be sure to keep a bandage on it." The women loved it. They called her "*La Bossa*" (the Boss Lady), and they acted like prima-donnas when "*La Bossa*" asked such personal, sensitive and caring questions.

Tom's father, although always there beside her when the crew arrived, never said much since he couldn't speak Italian and most of these women couldn't understand much English. My mother, therefore, wasn't just their supervisor. She was like the proverbial mother hen with her brood. She was their interpreter, their nurse, their care giver. At times, to me it seemed almost feudal. It wasn't really. It was a symbiotic relationship and all of them, not just my mother, were much more savvy than they appeared and did what they did, because they knew there would be a reward in the end. Great actresses, one and all. My mother took good care of her peelers and they, in turn, trusted and cared for her like loyal and faithful servants. "One hand washes the other," she'd say. She helped them with paper work since most could only manage a quivering "X" as a signature, they trusted her to count their dozens accurately and not cheat them, they trusted her to arrange with Mr. Dresser to stretch their work weeks or rearrange them if need be so that they could qualify for unemployment later in the fall. They simply trusted her. I guess they needed her as much as she needed them. She sincerely tried her best saying, "I remember what it was like when I first came over here."

If I didn't know Mr. Dresser was Tom's father, I never would have guessed it. They were as different as apples and oranges. Tom had glossy, dark hair and the darkest eyes I'd ever seen. Mr. Dresser had reddish hair and a fair complexion. If he ever got a bit of sun, he'd turn as red as one of his tomatoes, while Tom tanned beautifully to a divine chestnut colour. Tom took after his mother who, I'd heard, was part Indian, not Indian as in India but rather as native, aboriginal.

Mrs. Dresser was petite and consequently Tom was not quite as tall as his father but he was terribly handsome all the same. But Mr. Dresser, in spite of his reddish hair and fair complexion – a coloring not in favor in our family where all the men were dark – was a stunningly good looking man, although so different from my father who also turned heads with his thick, raven locks and neatly trimmed mustache like Clarke Gable. Mr. Dresser was also exceedingly charming and civilized, and what he lacked in coloring he made up for in stature, stance and comportment. In the morning, when he and my mother stood at the entrance to greet the workers, some of the younger women glanced appreciatively at this blazing auburn stallion, and I wonder now what thoughts were racing through their minds.

These morning sessions with my mother were meetings of sorts where she grilled me on how to approach my job, and instructed me like a stern but benevolent teacher.

I'd report. "Gelsomina's hair was unbearable today."

She'd say, "I'll talk to her. Can't risk having a food inspector walk in on us and sniff that."

"I asked what kind of shampoo she uses, just to see what she'd say," I'd continue. "You won't believe what she told me, and proud as a peacock too . . . She said she washed her hair only once a month or so because she didn't want to wash out the natural oils."

My mother laughs and shakes her pretty head. "Old country style, old country beliefs. But, listen, keep your eyes on her. She's not just a dirty person, she's a dirty peeler, a money hungry dirty peeler. I caught her trying to get away with slipping off the skins and not bothering to core."

Then she'd go on to explain the tactics I should use with people like Gelsomina. "Don't underestimate these women," she'd say, "especially types like her. You've got to outsmart them. Punch down the line and dump out and inspect a can or two from each woman. She'll have her eye on you and clean up her act expecting you at her spot. Then skip her and a few others and start punching somewhere else. She'll breathe a sign of relief and go back to her dirty ways. When she least suspects, go to her spot and dump a couple of cans."

"Trick her?"

"You have to. You have to watch them like a hawk." Then mellowing a bit she might add, "Oh, Lord, they don't mean to be troublesome. They just want to make money, especially someone like Gelsomina with Scrooge for a husband. Besides, they can't see what difference it makes if you leave some peel on." Then she'd straighten herself up and square her pretty shoulders and say, "But I have to be careful, see . . . If an inspector comes by to check and finds dirty cans, the whole day's production gets labeled Standard instead of Choice and then Mr. Dresser loses money . . . So, you see, it's all about money anyway you look at it."

As soon as the shiny cans, marching in formation like soldiers, clanked noisily, it meant reinforcements had been needed. The piercing sound of tin dropping down the chute was a signal for our meeting to break up. The peelers had little patience and would soon be clamoring for me to clear their work spaces and get their filled cans counted and out of the way. My mother would look up above our heads and say, "Go now. Get to work."

I'd sneak a peek up there too because it was Tom's job to commandeer the cans and load fresh troops on to the chute. Sometimes, a can or two broke ranks and got stuck sideways and the women would yell up at him. "*Disgraziato*," they'd shout, and I would turn red in embarrassment for the boorish and mercenary ways of the peelers, as well as for Tom's lack of care.

The cans jammed all too often, because Tom had his eyes on me down below, instead of on them. My mother had to run up and help him dislodge the little deserters far too many times, while the women below fumed and raged waiting for the cans to descend to be filled. The women would continue to peel leaving their naked tomatoes on their slippery counters. But many would fall making the factory floor treacherous. At times like this, everyone was in a panic, even Mr. Dresser, who could be seen with a push broom sweeping the sludge into the gutter. My mother transferred Tom to the warehouse, where he couldn't see me and had to stack cases instead.

That took away a lot of my fun, and I had to sneak out back to the warehouse to see Tom during breaks and lunch. Out there, in the midst of those mountains of neatly packed cases of tomatoes and surrounded by the intense pungent smell of cardboard, Tom and I stole fitful kisses and longed for time to stand still.

Late one afternoon, mechanical problems shut down the belts and all hell broke loose on the factory floor. The women yelled and shouted, some almost swearing with expressions I had only heard men use like "*Porca miseria*," "*maledetti*," and of course, the ever present "*disgraziati*." My mother was frantic, as was Mr. Dresser and the mechanics. Such lost time was lost money for one and all. It couldn't always be made up, because tomatoes were extremely perishable. I guess I was about the only one who thought this a stroke of luck, and I took advantage of the occasion to go out back to the warehouse and Tom. We were wild with yearning and lost track of the time and couldn't have cared less about what was happening in the plant. By the time I went back, the plant was empty and I dashed to the main entrance to see the rear end of the last bus pull out of the parking lot. I ran out and yelled for it to stop but, what with the noise of the bus, the exhaust fumes and all the irritated women cackling inside, no one noticed me. I had missed the bus. I looked for my mother's car, but it too was gone. I went into the lunch room and phoned my father to tell him I was going to stay on for the next shift not mentioning the reason why. "Has Mum been home?" I asked.

"No," he said matter-of-factly, "there's no sign your mother was here. No dinner even." I could hear him chewing on something, whatever it was.

His casual response sent a flash of anger through me. It was just like him not to show the least bit of concern for either of us: not for me nor my mother. Here I was, stranded and alone, at night, far from home, I didn't know where my mother was, and neither did he. But he didn't seem to much care about any of it. In fact, it was as if I was bothering him, and I could envision him just plopping the receiver down, while continuing to chomp on his supper and hastily flip through his newspaper before going out to play cards with his friends, as if this was just any other night.

Exhausted, I laid down on the couch in the lunch room next to the main office, worried about my beautiful mother all alone on some deserted county road with a flat tire or worse, while my father sat nonchalantly at a card table, smoking and sipping wine at the local club, and I guess I fell asleep.

At some point, I awoke, disoriented and confused, until I realized where I was and what had happened. Over the clanging and banging of the conveyor belts, which must have been repaired, my ears picked up sounds coming from the office. There was a door between the two rooms with a small pane of glass up top covered with a flimsy curtain. I stood up and went to peer into the office. Through the flimsy gauze, I saw my mother and Tom's father, he with his bright red head, nearly obliterating the view of my mother's dark curls which had escaped her hairnet, and I could make out the shape of his large hands undulating beneath her starched white dress and I watched her small, dark hands grip his wide shoulders.

I quietly went out the other door and scrambled up high in the warehouse where I stayed the rest of the night. Not that anyone would be looking for me. My father was convinced my mother would see me on the night shift; my mother was convinced I was home in bed. When it all came out in the wash next day, I'd just tell the truth and say I missed the bus and fell asleep and, when I awoke, decided to stay and wait for the day shift.

In the morning, when the night shift went home and there was this brief limbo before the day peelers arrived, I went back to the lunch room and laid on the couch to wait for my mother.

She bolted through the door as soon as she arrived having heard from the women I hadn't been on the bus. "Oh, my God," she cried. "Have you been here all night?"

I wasn't too sure if she was concerned about me, or if she was worried that I had seen and heard what I had seen and heard.

"I missed the bus last night," I said. That was all I said. I couldn't bring myself to utter another word.

"Where were you all night? Nobody said anything about you being in here."

"I slept in the warehouse," I said, thinking quickly. "Where I knew it would be quieter and I'd get some rest."

"Do you think you can work today?" she asked.

I nodded I could.

"I'll go get you a coffee and a doughnut," she said. And she was gone.

You'd think I'd be angry with her about the affair, but I wasn't really. After all, it was no different than what Tom and I were doing. I was angrier at my Dad. Angry that he was so blind, that he didn't have a clue, that he was so into himself that the thought would never have occurred to him.

In late fall, after the crescendo of feverish work had reached its climax and started to wind down, my mother's spirits appeared to take the same route and when the first snow fell and the cannery closed for the winter she seemed to resolutely settle into this new season's routine like a hunter waiting in his blind. Just before Christmas each year, there would be a flurry of activity when her peelers, like the Magi, dropped by with their homemade *pannettone*, *crostoli*, jars of preserves, and all manner of gifts. She'd glow contentedly and her spirits would pick up as with each visit she'd haul out her black binder of names and check off each gift bearer in preparation for next season.

My father hardly paid any attention to these intrusions, and if he happened to get the door when one came knocking, he'd just let her in and point to the kitchen, while he retreated to the living room and his easy chair. He never seemed to take notice how my mother was in a state of metamorphosis, fluttering, quivering and shimmying her way to freedom.

THAT SUMMER AT GRANDMA'S

When my grandmother calls to tell me about her dog, Sunny, she is weeping like a little girl. "Can you come down?" she asks between sobs.

This is the first time I have ever heard my grandmother cry.

"I'm on my way," I assure her, doing my best to rein in my own feelings. After all, Sunny was my dog too.

It's a good half hour drive to her small farm and, today, it will take longer because of the recent snowstorm. Although the ploughs have done a decent job, high winds blow the snow back on to the roadway almost as fast as it is cleared. This merciless flat landscape we live in has no compassion. When I finally arrive, I have dried my eyes but she is still crying.

Grandma has lived on this small plot of land ever since I can remember. When I was young, I spent my summers at her place. In those days, when my mother went off to work on the tobacco farms, I was regularly shipped off to Grandma's. My father was left behind in the city, but I don't think it ever occurred to any of them that he could have taken care of me.

Those were lean and hungry times when people had to fend for themselves for the most part. There weren't many government safety nets then, and if you didn't bring home the bacon, you generally didn't get to eat it, although that wasn't always the case, as I learned that one summer at Grandma's.

And so, when school ended in June, immigrant mothers like mine went off to the tobacco farms of Southern Ontario to work like slaves fifteen hours a day, seven days a week, all season long. These farms were a good half day's drive from the city we lived in, and out-of-town workers like my mother had no choice but to room-and-board there, leaving their children with relatives who, in turn, also reaped monetary rewards, although not as hefty. Mind you, I don't think Grandma got paid to take care of me. She wasn't that mercenary.

As I boil water to make tea for her the way she used to for me when I was under the weather, I find it hard to insert this frail, old woman into the frame of my childhood. The fact that she is crying over Sunny is an unexpected but welcomed surprise. Not that I enjoy seeing people suffer. On the contrary, I am no sadist. But her reaction is unexpected because she had always been a pillar of physical and emotional strength. And it is welcomed because it makes her more like me.

I haven't been coming out as often as I used to, but I still visit regularly enough because, as I said, Sunny was my dog too. He and his sidekick, Misty, were at the Stanner place that one summer when I was ten or so and they became our dogs – mine and Grandma's – through a rather peculiar set of circumstances.

The Stanners always had mutts coming and going. None ever seemed to last. They either got run over by a truck or disappeared mysteriously. Misty and Sunny, two alert and intelligent Heinz 57 types I became attached to, had lasted the longest. Probably because Marie Stanner, who seemed to be the oldest of the girls over there, had taken to tying them up to a pole in the middle of the yard most of the time. Much as I disliked them being chained like that, I knew it was best for their sake since the Stanners didn't have a fence around the property.

That summer at Grandma's, I'd only been there a few weeks when, one morning, I awoke to the sound of Misty and Sunny barking excitedly. I pulled on my clothes and went out to the front porch for a better view. My bedroom window at Grandma's was too high for me to see out properly and, even then, there wasn't much of a vista with the corn field between her place and the Stanners'. I noticed what appeared to be two more dogs. These two new ones were just lying there on the ground, not moving. It looked like they were sleeping. But when I spotted Misty and Sunny galloping around like just released convicts, I knew something was odd. They weren't tied to the pole, and they seemed to be going up to the ones that lay huddled on the ground, barking the way dogs bark when they're curious.

Grandma was already out back in her garden. She liked being there early before the sun got too strong. So I just slipped into the cornfield between the two farms.

I should mention these weren't real farms, Grandma's and the Stanner's next to us. Not great big spreads like the Paquette place across the road. That was a real farm. It had a long, low henhouse with hundreds of cackling chickens, a monstrous barn with dozens of milk cows, and a shed where everyday tall and shiny metal cans stood at attention waiting for the milk truck and my grandmother, whose job it was to load them into the large metallic vehicle. Grandma's place was just a few acres of corn one year, soy beans the next. The Stanners weren't farmers at all. They just rented out that house which belonged to the Paquettes and was where one of the Paquette sons used to live before he gave up on farming and moved to the city.

As I cut through the corn field that morning, big floppy

green leaves slapped me in the face. I stopped dead in my tracks when I got close enough to see those weren't dogs on the ground tied up to the pole in the middle of the yard. They were kids, like me. Maybe even my age. I just stood there with questions wanting to shout out.

Misty and Sunny kept jumping around crazy like. The two kids weren't resting or sleeping. They were huddled close and looked scared to death. They hadn't even noticed the dogs' wagging tails.

For a long time I stood there in the field letting the corn hide me. Finally, Marie Stanner came out her back door with two bowls. I crouched down on the ground because I didn't want her to see me. Marie whistled at Misty and Sunny. She walked to a makeshift dog house at the back of the yard and placed the bowls down for the dogs.

She and the dogs had to climb over piles of stuff to get back there. The Stanner yard was the messiest place I'd ever seen anywhere. A regular junk yard. Instead of grass and flowers and a vegetable garden, they had rusted old car parts, bits and pieces of motorcycles, wringer washers, push lawn-mowers, and rubbish everywhere. A regular rotting hard-ware store. There were soggy mattresses, old bed springs, wrecked furniture, and piles of old lumber with rusty nails sticking out every which way. There were dozens of window frames stacked up against a sagging old fence. Some still had a few panes of glass, others just shards that glinted when the sun shone.

I waited and waited, expecting Marie or someone else to come out and untie those two kids. I figured they were friends and this was some kind of joke. It had to be. But no one came out.

Just as I was about to get up and turn back into the corn field, Marie came out again. Two more bowls in her hands.

She walked over to the pole where the kids were tied up like dogs and she placed the bowls on the ground without saying a word. I saw the kids move, then they sat up and each one snatched up a bowl and ate whatever was in it with their fingers.

I remember running fast back through the corn field and going straight to Grandma's garden bewildered by what I had seen. "Grandma," I called all out of breath. "Grandma, there's two kids tied up like dogs over at the Stanner place."

Grandma didn't even look up when I said this. She just kept pulling weeds. "Never mind all that," she finally mumbled. "That's none of our business."

"But, Grandma," I persisted.

"But nothing. What they do on their own property is their business."

She straightened up when she said this and the look she gave me said I was to drop the subject.

None of it made any sense to me then.

After breakfast, Grandma used to send me over to the Paquette place to play with the kids there. Nana Paquette, as everyone called her, had a whole slew of grandchildren. Not just one like my Grandmother. Every summer, they took turns coming to the farm and I took turns playing with them. It made no difference to me which ones were there. We always had fun. When Jimmy and Lenny were around, we climbed up into the huge hay loft in the big barn and then jumped down into the lower level. Depending on what part of the summer we were in, we'd hitch a ride on the tractor when Mr. Paquette ploughed the fields or lie in the wagon and let the wheat coming off the combine chute bury us. Whatever. It was all fun. When the girls came, Jane and

Susan, we'd go into the hen house and collect warm eggs. Then we'd clean off the smelly chicken excrement with little damp cloths, being careful not to break the shells, and we'd pack the eggs into grey cartons. Nana Paquette was good at finding something for us to do if we got the least bit bored or if she thought we were getting into too much "mischief," as she called our playing. We could always dig up potatoes or snap dangling beans from her staked up plants or help her make pies, which was one of my favorite "chores." I loved the smell of cinnamon and apples baking and couldn't wait for the pies to cool and Nana Paquette to cut us a giant sized piece which she'd smother with whipped cream.

Jimmy and Lenny were visiting at that point and I sailed across the road dying to tell them about the kids tied up like dogs.

"Off you go now." Grandma would clap her hands and shoo me away the way she shooed her chickens. I knew she wanted to get rid of me, but I didn't care. It was more fun at the Paquette place anyway.

I would hardly be across the road when Glenn's car would pull into Grandma's driveway. Then the mailman would stop in and eventually a whole lot of other men would be by. Grandma did grow corn and soy beans and she had a great big garden and did odd jobs for the Paquettes. But those things weren't enough to live on, according to her. So she sold the wine she made from her very own vineyard and sometimes even her *grappa*, though she knew this was all illegal. "To take up the slack," she'd say. "Because you've got to fend for yourself."

She herself never touched the stuff, except to make sure it tasted alright and hadn't turned to vinegar, and it amazes me now to think she had no qualms about selling it, although I didn't give it much thought then. I hadn't questioned much of anything until that summer. When you're a child, you passively accept what's thrown at you, I've learned. No questions asked. Those come later. And the answers later still.

I found Jimmy and Lenny already up an apple tree, eating green apples. I waved them down. "Jimmy, Lenny," I yelled.

"Yeah, yeah, we know. Shouldn't eat green apples. We'll get sick to our tummies."

They jeered at me in unison and made their usual grotesque faces. "Who cares about that?" I replied. "Come down. I want to show you something."

"Oh, wow," Lenny said sarcastically. "Maybe she's finally going to let us look up her . . ."

"Stop it, you nincompoop," I shouted. "This is for real."

"I'll show you my snake if you show me . . . ," Jimmy tried to continue. But I put my hands on my hips and they came down pretty fast because they could see I meant business. Besides, they knew I knew they didn't have a snake and it was just their puny little dicks they wanted to show me.

"What's up, tight pants?" Jimmy said.

I didn't pay any attention to this silly talk. "There's these two kids tied up like dogs over at the Stanner place," I said. "Come on, I'll show you."

Jimmy and Lenny looked at each other and followed me.

"Pretend we're walking down the road, okay?" I said. "We'll duck into my grandma's corn field up there." I pointed up ahead where we'd be out of Grandma's view.

"Worried Grandma will see you?" Lenny taunted.

"She looks busy enough to me," Jimmy added. "There's cars in the driveway already."

I didn't pay attention to those remarks either. Didn't

their grandfather come over for a few drinks almost every night? Sure, I didn't want any of my city friends to know my grandmother sold wine and liquor and even beer. I'd figured that much out by then. But out here everybody knew and nobody seemed to make a big deal out of it. She was just kind of a hotel when the real hotels were closed.

We walked nonchalantly up the road and, when I was sure it was safe, we dipped into the field and raced through the rows of corn. Then there, at the edge of the field, we all stopped.

It was hard to tell if they were boys or girls or one of each. But it was easy to see they had choke chains around their necks and they were tied up to the pole where Misty and Sunny would usually be. They both sat there staring at nothing. They weren't talking to each other. Nothing. Just still and silent as statues. I couldn't understand why they didn't try to escape. Maybe they were too scared.

"Nuts," Lenny said.

"Told you," I added.

"Who are they?" Jimmy asked.

I shrugged my shoulders.

We went back to the orchard to climb trees. When we got tired of that, we went into the chicken coop and scared chickens until Nana Paquette came out and asked us to stop. "Your fooling with the chickens will get the poor creatures upset and then they won't lay eggs," she told us. "It is almost lunch time too."

Jimmy and Lenny had to go get cleaned up. And Mr. Paquette and the others would be coming in from the fields to eat. She always said I was welcomed to stay too, but I usually went back to Grandma's and ate lunch with her. Besides, after lunch I knew Nana Paquette always took a nap and we usually broke up about then anyway, since we couldn't do much playing while she rested, although sometimes, if we promised to do it quietly, she let us peel and core apples for the pies she made in the afternoon.

As I walked back across the road, I saw the Stanner car pull into their driveway. Mr. and Mrs. Stanner and Marie and two younger girls got out. They went to the trunk and unloaded groceries. I said a little prayer. "Please, God, let some of that food be for those two kids tied up like dogs."

Grandma and Glenn and the mailman didn't notice me coming in and I caught the tail end of their conversation.

"I keep my nose out of other people's business," Grandma was saying.

"But, Olga, it's sick."

"If you feel a compulsion to do something about it, be my guest. As for me, my good Samaritan days are over. If people don't meddle with me, I don't meddle with them."

When they saw me, they stopped talking the way grown-ups do when kids are on the horizon.

I didn't know then what I know now. That my grandfather had left her with three hungry mouths to feed: my mother, who wasn't a year old, her sister and a brother. He just up and left, never to return, never to send any financial assistance.

I ate scrambled eggs and toast in the kitchen by myself. Then I stacked a few bottles of beer in the fridge for Grandma and I put the empties back into their cases. Glenn and the mailman liked beer during the day and Grandma always kept a supply for them. As soon as I was done, I flew out the door saying I was going back over to play with Jimmy and Lenny, but I lied and went into the corn field instead.

Marie, her brother and her two younger sisters were out playing baseball. They had put Misty and Sunny in their dog house, so they wouldn't get in the way. The two kids were still just sitting there on the ground tied to the pole.

I ran back over to the Paquette place and asked Jimmy and Lenny to come play baseball at the Stanner's. That way we could get up close and see what was gong on.

We snuck around like before. Marie was glad enough to see us. We played like usual. As if the two kids weren't even there. Nobody said a thing. Sometimes I purposely hit the ball in their direction just to get them to move or do something. But they were like two store dummies. Once, a ball went right by them and all they had to do was stretch out and stop it, but they didn't.

That night I awoke screaming and tearing my grandmother's arms from me.

"It's okay," she said shaking me awake. "Just a nightmare."

I dreamed I had a choke chain around my neck and I was tied to a pole.

In the morning, Grandma could tell I was upset. She made my favorite. Pancakes. But that didn't help. I wouldn't talk to her. I kept my lips tight together like a clam. And although I did enjoy breakfast, she wasn't going to pry me open with pancakes smothered in butter and maple syrup.

She tried though. "I know you're upset about those kids," she started. "Those damned bums."

I didn't know who she was talking about. The Stanners, the kids?

"They come over here and buy beer and wine when they run out, then go home and drink till they're falling down dead drunk. There must be a dozen kids over there. No one seems to work. How do they live? You tell me? I heard those two new ones are foster children they got just so they can collect money. Some new government thing . . . Lazy bums. Wasn't like that in the old days. You learned to fend for yourself then. But, hey, none of my business how people choose to earn a living."

She wasn't really talking to me anymore. Just talking to herself. I finally gathered the "damned bums" were the Stanners, because they were always coming over and buying their beer or wine and drinking till they were dead drunk and nobody over there seemed to have a job. But questions were beginning to brew and take shape in my child's mind. Why, I wanted to ask Grandma, did she sell them the stuff?

When Glenn pulled in, I got up and cleared my dishes. Grandma went outside and I could see the two of them talking. He glanced over at the Stanner place, then went to the trunk and took out six cases of beer which he handed to Grandma two at a time and she brought them in. I always thought it kind of funny how Glenn bought the beer and Grandma paid him for it and then he'd just come in, sit down and drink it and pay her back double the cost one bottle at a time. I couldn't understand it just like I couldn't understand the kids tied up like dogs.

As usual, when Glenn hauled the last two cases out of the trunk, Grandma would look to see if one was a different brand, which it often was. "Hrump," she'd mumble. "Got the mailman what he likes, did you?"

"Now, Olga. It's just a few cents more a case," he'd say apologetically.

Then Glenn would go back to the car and get a still warm apple pie for me. He did this regularly, every time he went for beer. "For you, little girl," he'd say. I'd always smile and say thank you. He didn't know Nana Paquette's pies were so much better.

"And what am I?" Grandma would mutter when he handed me the treat. "Chopped liver?"

I liked Glenn. He was the nicest of all the men. Not that any of them were mean or bad. I just didn't like them sitting around day and night drinking. But at least most of them didn't get skunk drunk like the Stanners. Although the mailman did wet his pants a lot when he'd had too much. Then Grandma would get mad and send him home.

As I left the house, I told Grandma I was going to play baseball at the Stanner place. I ran out the door not waiting to hear what she had to say about that.

I marched over to collect Jimmy and Lenny and we went straight to the Stanner place and boldly knocked on the back door.

"Aren't you afraid your grandmother will get mad?" Jimmy teased.

"Nope," I answered confidently. I was allowed to play baseball over there, although I knew Grandma would have preferred I didn't.

I could see it was a boy and a girl now. They looked so much alike they had to be brother and sister. The blonde hair was ragged and dry looking. Their eyes had that far away stare again, as if they were looking at something the rest of us couldn't see. Their bowls were empty, so I knew they had had something to eat. I wanted to say hello to them, ask them their names, why were they here, why were they chained, were they afraid, cold, hungry, in pain? Did they have any parents, a grandmother, a friend? Were they angry? So many questions I wanted to ask them, but didn't dare. I almost didn't dare look at them, I felt so strange. Here I was free as a bird. There they were, chained to a pole.

I planned their rescue. When all the men were gone home and Grandma was asleep, I'd crawl out of bed, sneak out of the house, slip through the corn field and let the boy and girl free. I'd take off their choke chains and liberate them.

I was in bed by nine, but the night dragged on at a snail's pace. Grandma's bottle opener was working overtime. The chatter from the living room droned on into the night. When I awoke, it was daylight. I jumped out of bed and ran to the window. There they were. Still chained. I'd failed them.

I vowed I would not fall asleep again that night. I would pinch myself until it hurt every time I felt my eyes close.

But I failed them again and again, night after night. I couldn't stay up later than Grandma and the men.

I decided I had to get out of the house before I fell asleep. I would climb out the window. No one would notice. To be sure Grandma wouldn't come into my bedroom where she kept her stock of beer and liquor, I'd fill up the fridge after dinner. I didn't have to worry about the wine because it was in the cellar. She always took care of that herself, ever since I accidentally forgot to turn off a spigot and drained a demijohn.

That night, the moon was just a silver crescent in the sky and not much use to me, as I wove my way through the corn field and over to the boy and girl. I walked into the back yard. I didn't have to worry about Misty and Sunny hearing me.

With all that junk something was always rattling and making plenty of noise. Besides, they knew me well and wouldn't have barked regardless. There was the pole, but not the kids. They were gone. Only the chains remained. Where were they? I looked around fitfully and finally spotted them. They were lying on mattresses in the back porch of the house. No way I could get in there. There was a padlock on the door. My plan to liberate them at night was as unlikely as my becoming the Queen of England.

I went back to bed planning a new attack. I was like a dog with a bone. I would get Jimmy and Lenny to help me out. We would do it together. We would free the boy and the girl.

As I plotted and planned, the chatter in the living room froze for a moment and I listened with curiosity. Mr. and Mrs. Stanner had walked in. They were here, in my grandmother's house and they were going to buy liquor and get drunk as skunks for sure. Good, I thought. Tomorrow they'll have a hangover and sleep in. I knew about such things having seen Glenn and the others the day after they'd had too much to drink. I'd be able to go over there in the morning and do what I had to do. Do what no one else seemed willing to do.

I never did get my chance to become a big hero. In the morning, when Glenn arrived, he told Grandma how someone had found Mr. and Mrs. Stanner dead and drowned in their car turned upside down in the ditch over on the next concession.

"They were so drunk, they probably never knew what happened," Glenn said.

I ran outside in my pyjamas when I heard the news. Straight through the corn field and over to the Stanner place.

"Marlena," Grandma called. "Wait."

I didn't.

I was breathless when I got there, my eyes filled with tears of joy. They were free, I wanted to tell them. But they were gone. The choke chains were there and the leashes and the pole, but the boy and girl were gone.

Grandma, a big woman, came running up behind me, huffing and puffing. She was so out of breath she could hardly get the words out.

"They're okay," she said finally, gasping for air. "They're over at the Paquette place . . . And Misty and Sunny are out back . . . In our yard," she managed to add, afraid I hadn't understood. I raced over to Nana Paquette's home, not even realizing I was still in pyjamas until Jimmy and Lenny saw me and giggled. The two kids were at the kitchen table, gulping down a breakfast of bacon and eggs and pancakes smothered with butter and syrup. When Nana Paquette saw me, she just said, "Why good morning, Marlena. Won't you sit down and join us?"

I got to know their names: Jake and Judy. And the fact that they were twins and their mother had died of some dreadful disease a while back and they'd been in foster homes as long as they could remember. They didn't know anything about a father.

No one had adopted them yet because the agency wanted them to stay together and not too many people were willing to take on two kids.

Jake and Judy stayed at the Paquette place the rest of the summer. Nana Paquette had said there was plenty to do on a farm this time of year and as long as they helped out she was glad to have them.

Misty and Sunny ended up settling in at Grandma's. They seemed quite content in the old abandoned dog house she cleaned out for them back behind the tool shed, although they too, like me, spent a lot of time cavorting at the Paquette place. At the end of each day, when I crossed the road with Misty and Sunny at my side like guardian angels, I too felt quite content knowing Jake and Judy and the dogs would be there tomorrow, and all of them were safe and sound now.

By the end of the summer, when it was time for me to go back to the city and school, Jake and Judy had become my best friends. I was crying when I went to say goodbye, thinking the adoption agency would send them someplace else and I'd never see them again. Imagine my joy when Nana told me they would be staying. "There's always plenty to do on a farm," she'd said. "Even in winter."

When Nana Paquette died years later, Jake and Judy discovered she'd left them quite a nest egg. She'd set up bank accounts for each of them and had deposited there every penny the government agency had sent her for taking care of them. She hadn't touched a cent.

Misty and Sunny lived on at Grandma's for years, smart dogs that they were. Never got themselves run over. They became my summer dogs since I wasn't allowed animals at home in the city, pets being tantamount to parasites for my parents. And even when I outgrew my summer's at Grandma's, I visited faithfully.

Misty went first, a few months back, and today Sunny died, of a broken heart, I'm sure.

I pour Grandma a cup of steaming tea and add three spoonfuls of sugar the way she likes it. "Here, Grandma," I say, reverting to cliches. "It'll make you feel better." I hurt too and don't know what else to say right now. I shiver. I feel the chill of winter in this old house. Always frugal in these matters, she never kept it too warm. "Drink, Grandma," I say lifting the cup to her lips. "Warm yourself up before we go out."

After a couple of tentative sips, she whimpers, "They're all gone now . . . Glenn and the mailman, Nana Paquette, Misty and now Sunny. Everybody's gone."

"And what am I?" I chirp with forced good humor. "Chopped liver?"

She has to smile at that and when she looks up and our eyes meet, I feel we have both just acquired a pearl of wisdom. I can't help thinking how we must all be in a perpetual state of becoming. We are like a child's snowball being rolled about the yard gathering the freshly fallen flakes.

Under the reverent and watchful eyes of their offspring, we bury Sunny out back next to his beloved Misty in an abandoned section of the garden where the earth, though snow covered now, permits our shovels ingress. And I tell Grandma their spirits will be there to keep her company. When she looks up at me again, I can see she is wondering if this could be possible.

"And if that isn't enough," I say as I pick up one of the younger dogs, "There's this little fellow." My own cheeks damp with tears, I say, "Promise, Grandma. Promise you'll take care of him, 'cause as soon as I'm on my own, he's coming with me."

There are fewer flowers this year. That's the first thing I notice. I feel the guilt.

When she phoned earlier today, I was annoyed, as always. It was eight o'clock, Sunday morning. I went through the usual routine: Why does she always call *me*? Why does she always have that false sense of urgency in her voice? One week it's "come and get the fresh asparagus and bring me a few jars of coffee." Next week it's "the lettuce and I'm out of detergent."

Sometimes I mutter my protests to my husband, sometimes to my mother, but usually I just grumble to myself, frustration building in me, knowing I am impotent against her. I always obey. I know that's why she calls *me*.

I often think she uses the asparagus and the lettuce only as an excuse. What she really wants is to feel the power she has over me.

This thing about food is annoying. I have more important missions to pursue than to run down there to pick up a bunch of asparagus. She belittles my artistic pursuits, saying if I had grown up like her I wouldn't have had time for such "stuff."

Food has always commanded great respect for her. Food was the answer to everything. Depressed? "Eat! You'll feel better." A cold? "Hot milk with honey." Tired and listless? "Boiled barley."

My father always said food was just something you had to ingest in order to sustain the body. A necessary inconvenience. I guess I am of the same opinion. Not her. She is the kind who seems to live for that sort of pleasure of the palate. When she sits down to a meal, she sits down. She lingers over her food, savoring it in all its richness, like a horny old man looking at a delectable young body. Her own body is no such attraction. She is grotesquely overweight these days.

When she was young, she was always hungry, she says. She survived two world wars, and more than half her life has been spent trying to earn enough money to feed herself and her children.

"As long as you have something to eat, clean clothes, and your hair is neat and combed, what else could possibly matter?" she would say.

Love, I'd think.

There aren't any flowers around the pear tree. Usually she digs a doughnut shape of earth around the tree and she plants impatiens. I look at the rest of the yard. Things are missing.

I am happy to see she has planted geraniums in the two pots on the front porch. It hasn't come to that yet. The self-seeding flowers and perennials are there too, though she played no role in their resurrection. They just continue to multiply, will continue to do so even after she is gone.

The lack of her hand shows. The chicken coop is empty, the garden untilled.

The small, red-bricked house is now dwarfed by the spreading pines that once framed her front window, and I think it looks queer to see how they have grown while the house has remained the same. It is a tiny house: one room across the front with a kitchen at one end and a combination living room-dining room at the other. There are two tiny bedrooms and a bathroom. She says it's enough for one, and that's true.

Is she trying to tell the world something with this house? Is she trying to tell the world she needs no one?

When I was a little girl I used to love going to Grandma's. I approached my summers full throttle. Freedom and liberty were at hand. Grandma allowed me to do just about anything whereas my mother never allowed me roller skates or even a bicycle.

Grandma let me go to the farm across the road all day long, as long as I popped in for lunch and supper and came to bed when it was dark. The Paquette grange was a real farm. Hundreds of acres and all sorts of animals plus an assortment of grandchildren that came and went all summer long. Old Mr. Paquette and his three sons ran the farm. The place was always in a bustle, buzzing like a beehive. We collected eggs, wiping them with a damp cloth before gently nestling them into their containers. We cut the lawn and cleaned the farmhouse. Sometimes Mrs. Paquette – Nana, to one and all – would reward us with a slice of apple pie or maybe pumpkin with real whipped cream. Grandma always bought her pies from the breadman. Once, I asked her why she didn't make pies like Nana Paquette and she told me she never had the luxury of being able to make such things when she was in the old country. Consequently, she had never developed the custom. "Where do you suppose we would get the sugar?" she'd say. "We had trouble getting enough cornmeal to eat!"

On Sundays, my parents sometimes came down to see how I was doing. Naturally, I looked healthy. Kids generally do in summer after a dreary Canadian winter. It must be said, of course, Grandma always fed me well. "Why do you think I grow all this stuff?" she would say. "It's for you and for them," she'd point to my parents, "so you can eat decent food and not that store bought trash."

I remember one Sunday visit. I had just come home from church. The Paquettes, all of them, always went to church on Sundays, and Grandma insisted I go too. She herself never had time for church. My friends and I were playing in the Paquette yard, over by the shed Mr. Paquette was building. I stepped on a plank which had a rather long nail sticking out. My little Sunday sandals didn't stand a chance. I remember how I cried and laughed. It looked weird, as if I had a platform beneath my foot.

Old Mr. Paquette came out and yanked the plank off and Nana sat me down in the kitchen and put my foot in hot, salted water. Dark red blood oozed from the wound and swirled around in the pail.

As I sat there I saw my parents drive up to Grandma's across the road and Nana Paquette made me promise to tell my mother so I could be taken for a tetanus shot. Naturally, I didn't tell her. I could have died, I suppose, but I would rather have died than have to tell her or Grandma about the nail.

I walked as best I could and mother noticed my gait was odd. I told her I had stubbed my foot on a rock. Grandma jumped in protectively. It wasn't all out of concern for me; it was for herself too. "What are you worried about?" she snapped defiantly. "A little thing like that! Why don't you look at her face and see how's she's filled in! Look at those skinny legs and how they're fattening up." She and my mother never got along.

I didn't see the discord until I was older. Grandma always talked about the wonderful presents she used to lavish upon my mother and my aunt. Every Christmas and Easter she sent them clothes and once in a while a real toy.

"They were the best dressed children in town!" she would say.

" . . . The only ones without a mother and a father," my mother would say when we talked about her youth. Oh, she would verify it was all true about the gifts, but the tone said something else.

"When did you ever see her?" I asked my mother once.

"Very rarely," she had replied. "She went away to work. Our father had gone to America and forgotten all about us. So I guess she had no choice. She sent us money and clothes, but we rarely saw her. You couldn't blame her, I suppose. One trip home and she would have used up all her savings."

When her two daughters were old enough to work, she had managed to find them employment with a well-to-do physician in Fiesole, a little town in Tuscany, not far from Florence, which was where Grandma worked as a housemaid. They saw each other more then, since they were closer, but it was still difficult. With only one day a week free, it was not easy to get to Florence from Fiesole and back.

When the Second World War began, she and my mother and my aunt walked and hopped on trains until they miraculously made it home.

During the war, that was the only time they lived together. Then, after the war, mother met father and they left the old country and my aunt met my uncle and did the same. It wasn't your regular family set up and I can see why love is lacking now.

My mother says she's just glad she had a wonderful grandmother who loved her and took care of her all those years. When I hear this, I think about my feelings for Grandma and I try to understand how and why I lost my love for her. I loved her once, as a child. I know I did. I must have. But it is gone. Since one particular incident.

I was about twelve. Mother was working on a tobacco farm that summer and Grandma was with us. I was at that awkward age, a girl sprouting into a woman. And all the visible signs of womanhood were being cast upon me. This tormented me to no end. Breasts were such a bother. How uncanny that I should grow such vulgar appendages. In a household where things of the body are kept secret, it was a curse to have been given visible proof of growing up. It was an enormous burden for me to have to parade around with two little lumps the size of marbles beneath my clothes. Consequently, I always walked around slightly stooped and Grandma shouting, *"Stand up straight!"* only made me hunch up more.

So, when I wore that loose fitting blouse with the long sleeves to wash the basement stairs, I was only trying to camouflage my transforming body. How could I explain to Grandma that I was ashamed? I didn't even know it myself. All I knew was that I felt uncomfortable.

She got upset with me for being so foolish. She was right, of course. It was foolish to try to wash the stairs wearing a shirt with sleeves that dipped into the pail.

She told me to tuck the shirt in and roll up the sleeves, for heaven's sake! Didn't I see I was getting soaked! I wouldn't listen. She got angry and told me to just take the shirt off. She tugged at my soaked clothing. The thought horrified me and I ran from the house, leaving my work unfinished.

Things have never been the same since.

Perhaps I was too sensitive or she wasn't sensitive enough. After all, she hadn't gone through the perils of having to actually raise her children; her mother had taken up the task for her.

A few years ago she stopped keeping ducks. "Why bother?" she had said. "It's just more work and my legs are getting weak and my shoulders hurt." She still had the chickens and the garden. I could still enjoy the feel of a smooth, still warm egg reached from beneath a trusty hen.

I can still see her walking out to the chicken coop with her bucket of feed, calling to her hens as they came clucking along. She used to say they knew her, they trusted her.

I began to see a pattern. The way she was with her animals, that's how she was with young children. She was gay around them. She seemed to sincerely enjoy their presence. She gave to them, as she gave to her animals and to the growing things around her. She gave endlessly, barring no expense, asking for only a kiss in return.

Being what they are, they gave the kiss willingly and with unabashed candor.

Perhaps it is knowledge that kills love. Perhaps it is growing up. I started to see things I had never seen before and question others I had never questioned before. I started to want to know the truth, as if that would bring anything but sorrow and pain.

With my own feisty little son, she is as she used to be with me. I watch her and I remember. Her old eyes light up, and I feel the guilt. Why can't I love her? What has she ever done to me that is so unforgivable? Innocence lost, I lost love.

Why can't I remember the good things? The gold watch she sent me from Montreal when she worked there as a maid. The play set of table and chairs that came that Christmas. The typewriter she gave me when I started high school. All expensive gifts for a grandma who worked on her hands and knees. She had done the same for her own children. Sent them things. Expensive things. Things no one else had.

The chickens went soon after the ducks. That upset me. It was the way she did it. She enlisted us one Sunday – mother and I and my aunt – and she had us slaughter all the hens! Just like we used to in the old days when we first arrived from the old country. She and my aunt stuck sharp knives into their skinny throats and held them upside down to drain the blood as they flapped wildly. One after the other, they slaughtered them. We boiled water, plucked and cleaned them, bagged them, and prepared them for the freezer. Mother and I, more squeamish than the two of them, could handle that part.

She was as unattached as a butcher, showing no feeling for the animals she had fed and watered through cold dreary days or hot, humid ones, the animals who were her only companions for days at a time, the animals who trusted her. When it was over, she said: "Well now, the three of you can divide them up and take them home. You have enough to last all winter."

She was practical. She simply couldn't handle the work any longer. Just walking to the chicken coop had become a chore.

The garden went a few years after that. Last year, all she had were a few tomatoes and some beans. This year the ground has not been broken.

I guess I knew this would be one of my last trips down there. Perhaps she knew it too and perhaps that's why she looked through me as she did. It is a replay. I always feel the anguish as I leave the house. It is only when I am nestled inside my car and a safe distance away that I can actually look her in the eye. Otherwise, I avoid her gaze. And she used to avoid mine too. Lately, however, I've noticed she looks at me with something in her eyes. I would call it innocence if it were in someone else's eyes. I don't know what it is, but she looks at me in such a way and the hurt penetrates. Does she know how I feel?

I wonder if she'll change now that she's near the end?

When her brother died last year, we hesitated to tell her. We never learn. We always think this one is going to get to her, but it never does. We keep on giving her the benefit of the doubt. Maybe we do it more for ourselves than for her. After all, she is our blood. When we told her, she just put on that false sorrow of hers which we recognize immediately and we are hurt. The next time we went down, she didn't even mention it.

It was the same when the Paquettes died. It was strange, since old Mr. Paquette was actually younger than Grandma. When he died, she said: "Oh well, what can you expect at his age." She never thought of herself as old. Not until recently.

For years she had worked for the Paquettes. I remember her walking across the road to load the milk containers onto the milk truck. Old Mrs. Paquette could never lift such weights.

Work never frightened her. She had worked ever since she could remember. It was by scrubbing other people's floors and washing other people's dirty laundry that she managed to scrimp and save to buy the tiny farm and this house.

She says she's never had it so good and, I suppose, she hasn't if you compare this to what she had before. It's just that I would have expected much more. She says we all expect too much these days. I don't mean that I would expect more in terms of material things; no, I expected more emotionally. I couldn't see myself living alone, year after year, the way she does, without a man.

She was only in her twenties when he left her and, as far as I know, she has never had another. I figured she was too old fashioned to get involved with a man while her husband was still alive. When he died, Grandma was in her sixties. My father joked about how she could go out now and find herself a man. I had taken my father's remark seriously. She had just moved out to that desolate little house, and I didn't know how she would be able to live there alone. She managed, however. She managed for well over thirty years.

All she ever said was that she didn't need a man. What had her husband ever done for her? Only leave her with problems.

It seems we stay less and less each time we go. She asks if I want coffee. Usually, I tell her to sit still; I'll put on the pot. These days it's such an ordeal for her to make coffee for more than herself. This time, I tell her I don't want any and she doesn't say much. She just looks around and asks when I'll be down again.

Her body is slowly deteriorating, leaving only an alert brain.

A few weeks back, when we all went down, she was so flustered we decided not to do that to her again. She was exasperated with having to open a bottle of beer for my father and my husband. "Get your own glasses," she mumbled. "My shoulder hurts when I raise my arm." She sat down and said an astonishing thing. Something I never thought I'd hear her say. "I'm tired," she said. "I'm tired of living."

She wasn't speaking to us or to anyone in particular. She just said it, and we understood.

We were touched by her feelings. Only my father knew how to change the mood. "So you want to die on us, do you? I hope you live to be a hundred," he said in jest. "That way we'll get all that pension money."

Such statements exasperated my mother. Even though she couldn't feel love for the woman, she still stubbornly displayed a sense of decorum.

Grandma said she was planning on living to a hundred just to spite him. And then she amazed us with another unexpected remark. "And don't be so sure you're going to get all of my money," she said. "I've made out a will."

We knew she still had a tidy sum which she insisted on sharing with us: one of the few things that still gave her some satisfaction. In her mind, as long as she had money, she had power.

She must know she can't buy our love! She must! I guess she does, but she also knows us. She knows we can't refuse her gifts and she also knows once we have accepted them, we have an unsigned contract that says she can interfere with our lives. She holds us to her the way she held her children when they were young: with materialism. She knows no other way.

Now Grandma has made out a will. Everyone calmed down and a sort of reverence surrounded her – an aura. We all looked at her inquisitively, asking questions with our eyes. It was as if we were looking at a ghost and we waited for it to speak.

"I made out a will and you'll see it when I'm dead."

My father had tried for years to get her to do just that. She would have no part of it. "As soon as you make out a will, you die," she would say. Reasoning never helped. When Father would tell her that her life savings would be taken by the government, she would say, "I don't care who gets it!" Mother would cringe at such remarks.

I suppose she has had to adapt. She has had few choices. She has had to develop a tough skin. But it's that lack of need, that self-sufficiency that I hate the most.

So, this day, as I pull out of her driveway, I think about the will and I think about how this place will look when she will be gone. As I turn my head to guide the car out, I catch a glimpse of the old Paquette place across the road and the image remains in my mind all the way home: tall grass that needs cutting, weeds overgrowing the flowers, a broken pillar on the front porch, and peonies trying to survive.

"I do too have royal blood in me!"

"You do not!"

"I do too!"

"Do not!"

"I do, I tell you, I do! My father said so."

"Well, my father said you don't, so there."

"Look, my great-grandmother was a Countess. She had royal blood."

"You don't. You're not a Countess."

"But she was. Okay, so she married an ordinary man. That's the only reason she lost her title. If she'd married royalty, her children would have had a title too."

"But she didn't, and they don't."

"No, but, the blood . . . It was royal before she got married and it stayed royal even after she got married. I have some of her blood and so I have royal blood too. Don't you understand?" I pleaded.

Susan went off laughing at me. Marsha and Theresa, who hadn't said a word throughout the argument, snickered and followed Susan. I was left there, alone.

This sort of thing happened a lot when I was young.

My father used to tell me about our ancestors in the old country and I used to sit and listen. Later, I would lie awake at night trying to visualize my great-grandmother sitting in her polished carriage. It was drawn by two white horses and she held a frilly, silk parasol above her elegantly coiffed tresses. That's how she used to travel.

Even though she married a farmer, she never touched soil. Her hands were white and delicate, my father used to tell me.

Her family had a crest and the crest is still there above the doorway that opens into their big house. It is carved out of wood. There's a lion standing on his hind legs and he's wearing the headgear that knights in armor used to wear in the middle ages. I always found that rather amusing: a lion that looks like a knight.

Everything my father told me was true. It wasn't fictitious. But no one believed me. They laughed.

I remember the first time I went back to the old country, I couldn't wait to get to my home town. I desperately wanted to go to the cemetery to see my great-grandmother's grave. I wanted to see her picture, to see if she really was as beautiful as my father had said she was, and she was. He hadn't lied at all. I wasn't disappointed. On the contrary, I was proud.

I can still see her clearly. She is wearing one of those corseted dresses with a very high and ruffled neck. She has a large-brimmed and very ornate hat on her elaborately arranged hair. She is more beautiful than any other woman in the cemetery. All the others look old and shabby in comparison, their hair hidden with dark, patterned scarves which are tied behind their heads and sit low on their foreheads. Their faces are wrinkled; their mouths pursed for lack of teeth. Not my great-grandmother. She is wearing a hat.

Even in death my great-grandmother and my great-grandfather make a stunning couple. Most of the other couples look mismatched and peculiar. The women look aged and it seems preposterous to believe that these women were once married to the men whose photographs adorn the twin grave. The men look so young. That's because most died young. They didn't come back from wars, or they died in some distant land while struggling to earn a living in a mine or in some dingy factory or other. My great-grandparents lived long lives, together.

My great-grandfather was impressive looking, even though he was a farmer. But he was an affluent farmer with acres and acres of land and a stable bursting with horses. For thirty years he was mayor of our little town.

So great-grandmother had married an "ordinary man" only in the sense that he didn't have any royal blood. The closest he had come to royalty was the eight years he had spent as bodyguard to an Austrian Emperor. That was when our part of the country was under that country's rule. He had been selected because of his physical resemblance to the Emperor and also because he spoke the Emperor's language. Photographs of my great-grandfather in uniform – sword at his side and all – made him a dashing specimen indeed!

My father used to spend hours and hours talking about his grandparents and his parents, and how it used to be in the old country. I could never figure out why he and my mother came over here when things seemed so idyllic back there.

My father had another passion. Reading. He would read old books and I remember how it used to impress me when he'd summon me to him and he would insist I listen to this or that passage.

One of his favorites was a book about Julius Caesar. He loved the section on how Caesar had come up with the calendar that was the model for the calendar we use today.

"Read this," he'd say. And I would obey.

Later, when I was older, I would get belligerent.

"I don't want to read it, Daddy. I've read it a million times before."

He would shut his book forcefully and retreat to another part of the house, telling my mother I was insolent and not interested in "culture."

His "library" is the same today as it was thirty years ago. He still reads the same books over and over again. I don't recall him ever buying a book. The only new books he ever pored over were books my sister and I used to buy him, but even they weren't "new" because they were always books about his favorite characters or places: Caesar, Rome, Mussolini, Michelangelo, Da Vinci . . . It's almost as if he's been reading the same books all his life.

The Countess had two daughters: Ida, who was just like her mother, and Caroline, who was just like her father. The latter was my grandmother, my father's mother.

Caroline was tall and slim. By no means did she have the sophistication of great aunt Ida, her sister, nor the elegance of her mother, the Countess.

My grandmother, Caroline, had eight children, Father being one of them. Two died young. Caroline was a worker. She took care of the children, the house, the cows, the chickens, the pigs, the garden. Everything. She took care of everything.

Grandfather concerned himself with weightier and more momentous matters. Eventually, he took his father-in-law's place as mayor of the town and he was active in the politics of the region. He had little time for domestic affairs, children, and other such trivialities. He had more important missions to accomplish.

On that first trip back to the old country, I met Anna. She was the old woman who ran one of the local bars. I remember how striking she was even though she was old. Her hair, in the mode of a Spanish dancer, was pulled back into a magnificent bun which adorned the nape of her neck. Because of the natural wave of her raven locks, the tightly pulled strands undulated on her crown, despite the fact they were gathered to from the bun. Her eyes were black as night; her skin, fair, unlike most other women from those parts.

She talked endlessly about the old days. That was why I went to see her every day. I wanted to know more about my royal great-grandmother, but Anna seemed more interested in my father's father, Caroline's husband. That was okay with me too. I wanted to know everything about everybody.

She would tell me how important my grandfather used to be and how handsome and how witty.

Only recently did I find out Anna had been my grandfather's lover for thirty years. My father never told me that.

Another argument.

"We used to be rich before we came here. My father said so."

"So why did you come?"

"It was because of the war. We lost a lot during the war."

"Sure you did."

"We did. My father said so."

"Yeah, and I'm the Queen of Sheba."

Off they'd go again, their laughter echoing away from me.

I never told me father about these arguments. As a matter of fact, I never told him I used to talk about the things he used to talk about.

As I got older, I asked more questions. My father always answered my queries regarding our family's history, but I always felt cheated after one of these question and answer sessions.

"Daddy, if Grandpa had so much land and so much money, how come we came over here?"

"He had a lot, but he had to divide it into six parts because there were six of us who had to share it all. It really didn't leave much for any one of us."

It made sense, but for some reason I thought that if you come from a rich and almost royal family, that family should remain rich and almost royal. Why did it all have to come tumbling down?

"Daddy, why didn't any of you go on to university?"

"Your grandfather wanted us to go, the boys that is – he didn't believe in girls going to university – but none of us wanted to, that's all. Your uncles wanted to farm and I wanted to become a mechanic. I've always been interested in machines."

That always bothered me. How could the son of a rich man want to become a mechanic? Didn't mechanics come from a different class of people? I was confused. My father had always made it sound as if there were ordinary people in this world and then there were the others – like us. According to him, all the other mechanics he worked with fell into that ordinary category.

Then there was that statement about girls and university. I intended to go on to university. What would my grandfather think about that?

When Grandpa died, my father sold everything his father had left him. He owns nothing in the old country now. It's still all there, but it doesn't belong to our family anymore. I could never understand that, never.

"Daddy, why did you sell everything Grandpa left you? Why didn't you keep some of it, just as a memento of the past?"

"Oh, there wasn't much, really. And it wasn't worth anything anymore. That house was ready to fall apart. It would have cost too much to fix it up. And the land, well, there wasn't much land."

Our old house. I remember it well. It was over three hundred years old. I figured, if it had lasted that long, why couldn't it last another three hundred years? There are all sorts of buildings in the old country that are much older than that!

And the land. There's so little of it left in the old country you'd think every square inch would be worth its weight in gold. How could it be "hardly worth anything?"

He always used to talk about going back there to live, when he got enough money. Once, we nearly did. It was when I was thirteen years old. He sold our house and most of the furniture. We started packing the rest. I remember my mother crying continuously and vowing she wasn't going back.

Her memories of the old country were so different from my father's. "All I remember is being poor and hungry and never having enough meat," she'd say. For some reason I never really listened to her version of the old country.

He doesn't talk about going back anymore. I guess it's because he doesn't have anything to go back to. Except . . . his mother and his father, his grandfather, the mayor, and all the other people that made up his past.

As for me, I couldn't obliterate them all. He had made them too real. I went back as soon as I finished university. I got a job and lived there for a year, to the day, 365 days.

I used to go and see my birthplace often, my home, but it wasn't my home anymore. Father had sold it. I would visit my ancestors in their graves, but there weren't any more niches in the family plot.

I would go see our garden, where the chestnut tree still stands and bears fruit, but I couldn't pick a chestnut from the tree because it wasn't mine anymore.

During one of my visits to my village I got up enough courage to tell my grandfather I had finished university and I was now a teacher. I wonder what he would have said if he had been alive?

Years later, when I married, it was to someone from the old country. When his father died, he left us a sprawling old house, a barn for the animals, some land, and a beautiful garden complete with fruit trees. There isn't a chestnut tree in this garden, but the next time we return for a visit, we're going to plant one. Then I'll be able to pick my own chestnuts.

I remember, once, I asked my husband if there was any royal blood in his family.

"Yes," he said, "there was a duchess or something, somewhere back there, but it was a long way back."

He sounded glib and almost irreverent, and I chastised him as I continued my mission to disinter and salvage my nobility. "What about a crest?" I asked insistently, like an inquisitor.

Yes, he seemed to recall a family crest, but then "almost everyone in the old country had a family crest, didn't they?"

I wanted to know if they still had the actual crest itself. Was it carved in wood or stone?

It was neither, as it turned out. What it was, was a large painting of the family crest. The original, lost to time, had disappeared.

I worried the painting would be ruined or destroyed now that his father was gone. The thought obsessed me. It tormented me so much that my husband wrote to his sister and asked her to get the painting out and hang it in the entry hall, then take a picture of it and send it to me immediately.

I remember the excited flutter that gripped me when I finally received the photograph.

A ridiculous thought entered my mind as I slit open the envelope. Maybe now that I had married someone who was also "almost royal," as I had been, maybe now I was a little closer to having real royal blood?

The union of two people whose forefathers were of another class, does this produce what has been lost through the years?

My husband smiled at my hypothesis. "And even if it did," he said, "our children would surely lose it, just as surely as we have lost it ourselves."

"I saw two today."

"Two what?"

"Two moose."

"Where?"

"Down by the lake."

"What happened?"

"Nothing."

"What do you mean *nothing*?"

"Just what I said: nothing."

"Did they get away?"

"No, it wasn't like that."

"What happened then?"

Michael sat down at the kitchen table. He sank his head into his hands. "They practically walked into me. I was sitting in the truck when I thought I'd heard crackling sounds. I turned around and there they were, just a few yards away. They hadn't seen me, but I'm sure they had smelled me because they just stopped for a minute, facing my direction."

"What did you do?"

"I couldn't believe it. They were so close. I raised my gun to shoot. I could have had them both. I had all the time in the world to aim. They just stood there, not really sure if they were in danger or not. They couldn't see me, I'm sure. They may have spotted the truck, but they couldn't have seen me.

You know how bad their sight is. I aimed for the cow, the mother, but I couldn't shoot."

"You mean you didn't kill her?"

"No... I couldn't."

"Oh, Michael, I love you!"

"I knew you'd be happy." He looked up at his wife. He saw gentleness in her face and, for a moment, he was glad he hadn't killed the moose.

"Why are you so sad? Are you sorry now you didn't do it?"

"No, no. I didn't want to kill her. When I saw the two of them there, close to me, they looked so innocent. I thought about the little one. What would he do without his mother?"

"Why the glum face?"

"Because no one will believe I saw them. I know you do, but no one else will. If I saw the moose, I should have killed them. If I didn't kill them, then either I didn't see them or I missed them. They'll laugh if I tell them I was that close and I couldn't shoot. They'll laugh because I couldn't shoot. If I tell them I did, they'll laugh because I missed. No matter what I say, they'll make fun."

"It doesn't matter what they think."

"I know, but . . . "

"But nothing. You saw them and you didn't want to kill them. Why can't you just tell the truth?"

"Honey, wake up, wake up! Someone's out there. They threw something at the window."

"It's okay. It's just Nick and Jim."

"What are they doing here at this time of night?" Marlena reached for the clock. "It's four in the morning. You're not going hunting, are you?"

"Go back to sleep, honey." Michael sprang from bed and hurriedly threw on some clothes. "I'll be back in a few hours."

"You told them! You actually told them, didn't you?"

"No, not really. I didn't say I saw them. I just told them I saw tracks."

The three of them came back just as Marlena was sipping her morning coffee. They were in a bad humor. Nick looked wild. He was shouting. Marlena saw rage in his dark eyes. A big man with the musculature of an ox, he looked more fearsome than ever right now.

"Look, I tell you I hit her. She went down. I saw her head go down. Then I ran out of ammunition and you guys were far off. So I went over to where she was and I started giving it to her with the butt of my gun, right on the head."

He went through the motions as he told the story.

"She still kept trying to get up, the bitch. I was giving it to her as hard as I could and she'd just lift her head and try to pull herself up. I thought of the knife. I went to the truck to get it and, so help me, she wasn't there when I got back. She'd managed to get up and stagger away. I followed her tracks. She was bleeding like mad, but she went into the bog, and I lost her."

Rivulets of perspiration trickled down his face. He was livid. More so with himself and the moose than with Michael and Jim who had ripped into him for having lost her.

"Arguing isn't going to help," Michael said when finally their disappointment began to subside. "We'll go in this afternoon and look for her again."

They calmed down and agreed with him.

"Go on home and get a dry change of clothes. We'll meet back here later."

"Was it the same one?"

"I think so."

"Why, Michael? Why?"

"Leave me alone!"

"But she's out there suffering. You can't just leave her like that."

"What do you want me to do? Follow her through the bog? You know I can't do that. Just leave me alone, will you?"

They all looked fresh when they left the second time. They looked confident. Nick twisted his bulky torso towards Marlena before hopping into the truck, the only gesture any of them had made indicating they were aware of her presence.

"Don't worry none," he said. "We'll get a moose for you, my dear. Won't be back till we've got her. That's a promise."

They were doing it for her? Had they gone mad!

Michael slammed his door shut and revved the engine. He didn't look at his wife.

From the way they pulled into the driveway, Marlena knew they'd been successful this time. Their faces told the rest. Michael whisked his wife off her feet and twirled her round and round, shouting: "We got one, we got one."

"Put me down, Michael," she pleaded. "Put me down."

"Get us a beer, will you. We deserve it!"

They were jubilant. Marlena couldn't believe how much racket three men could make. They were reliving the hunt with each movement, each gesture, each word.

"Jesus Christ. When I saw her, I just knew, I knew she was mine," Nick bragged making it obvious he'd been the sharpshooter.

"I've got to hand it to you, Nick, you brought her down like a pro," Michael acknowledged excitedly. "She fell with the first shot," he told his wife. "Wait till you see her. What a piece of meat."

They could barely contain their euphoria as they discussed their strategy for bringing the animal out of the woods. They had left her there, dragged her into a thickly wooded area so no one would spot the carcass from the air. They hadn't bled her or opened her. Couldn't take the chance. They had gotten out fast. Poaching was a serious offence. None of them had a licence yet and, besides, moose season was a few weeks off. The area was patrolled routinely. Someone could have heard the shots and gone in to investigate. You couldn't risk getting caught. Game wardens would make you pay stiff fines and they could take the truck. So the men had hidden the moose as best they could and scrambled back to safety.

They had to figure out how to get at the carcass, but without the added risk of someone spotting the big red truck.

"We'll get your wife to drive us in," Jim said.

Nick didn't go for that. "No, it's no good having a woman in like that." He looked over at Marlena as if she was a blight on the landscape.

His dismissive sneer annoyed her. She felt insulted yet relieved at the same time.

"Why not?" Jim said. "She can drive us in and drop us off, then leave. We can clean up our moose without having to worry about the truck."

Michael looked at his wife trying to decipher her reaction. He knew perfectly well she was hardy and adaptable and not one to drawback if she had to get dirt under her nails. But had he gone out-of-bounds with this? Not quite certain what he saw in her eyes, he suggested a better idea. He would drive the two of them in, leave them there, and return later to pick them up. It wasn't necessary to have three people to gut the moose and divide her into quarters. They weren't intending to drag her out then anyway. They would do that later, when it was dark and there was less chance of being nabbed.

Marlena's face flushed as a glimmer of tenderness swept through her. Michael was willing to forego the hunter's pleasure for her sake. It was obvious, however, he ached to go with Nick and Jim. He had never been in on an actual kill before. She knew all he needed was a signal from her.

"It's okay," she said. "I can drive you guys in."

"Atta girl," Jim said. "You can drop us off along the gravel road. We can walk the rest of the way. Give us half an hour or so, then come back. We'll probably be done by then and we'll meet you in the same spot where you drop us off."

Nick didn't like the idea but went along since he couldn't offer an alternative.

Michael thanked Marlena with an uncertain smile.

It had been drizzling all day. Fog lingered in the sky. Some of it hung so low they cut through it with the red truck.

"Even the weather's with us," Nick laughed. "With this fog, no one will see us. I bet the helicopters aren't even flying."

They gave Marlena directions, but she didn't need them. She knew the area well. In the summer, she and Michael had gone hiking in there. They had fished in a gurgling stream and picked blueberries in the clearing not far from the lake. She even knew the trail that led to where the dead moose was hidden. She had picked wildflowers along there.

Marlena hadn't been in the woods since summer. The once green palate had transformed into shades of yellows and browns, and brilliant reds peeked out like signposts demarcating the route. The rain brought out the pungent scent of pine. It battered the pick-up harder and harder as it intensified. Little puddles became miniature lakes. Like thousands of long-nailed fingers, branches scratched the sides of the truck. The road became narrower and narrower, almost tunnel-like, the farther in she went. When she reached the trail, she stopped.

"Come on, honey, why don't you drive on in?" Michael coaxed his wife. "It's pouring. Besides, you'll be able to see the moose."

"You're going to get wet anyway in a few minutes," Marlena said as the three men beckoned her with their stares to go on.

"I know," Michael admitted, "but why get more drenched than we have to?"

"Come on, Lena. Be a sport." Jim joined Michael in pleading for a longer ride. She hated it when he called her Lena.

"You've never seen a real moose before, honey. Come on in with us. Take a few pictures."

Nick snickered. "You've come this far, you might as well go all the way," he said. "It'll be a real experience for you, unless, of course, you're scared of a hunk of meat."

Marlena maneuvered the vehicle into the narrow, muddy, trail. Primitive curiosity, and something else – she didn't know what – made her do it. This, she thought, must be what Eve must have felt in the garden of Eden with the serpent daring her to give in.

When they got to the spot where they had shot the moose, the men jumped out, not giving Marlena time to shift the truck into neutral. She turned off the ignition and followed. Her feet sank into the waterlogged earth; moisture seeped into her boots. Gushy sounds accompanied each step she took. A watery hole ambushed her and one foot disappeared. At the sound of her gasping, Michael reached out for her. She took his hand and let him lead her on. Twigs and branches caught her sweater. They were holding her back, almost as if they didn't want her to enter this private domain. Her jeans were wet to the knee. She kept her eyes glued to the ground and yet she still tripped over fallen branches and mounds of soggy earth. Was this the same terrain she'd traipsed through all summer long as sure footed as an elk?

Suddenly she heard Nick's triumphant voice. "Here she is," he said. Michael let go her hand.

Marlena raised her head and found herself staring into a big, wide-opened eye. She was no more than six feet away from the dead cow.

The men scurried about trying to decide how best to perform the job at hand, clicking pictures as they talked and scampered around the corpse. Nick plunked himself down on the big cow while Jim took a picture. Then he stood up and placed a foot on her abdomen smiling a lascivious victory smile. He looked like one of those guerilla fighters commonly seen on news footage. He took the camera while the others posed. They retrieved their guns which had been cautiously hidden beneath some fallen branches. More pictures: guns in hand. More screen footage for her.

Marlena stood frozen in her tracks. She couldn't move. There was blood everywhere. The moose had a gaping hole in her neck, another in her spine, and a third had shattered one of her legs.

The hair was brownish black in color, generously sprinkled with grey. It was thick and course and much longer than Marlena had imagined.

Michael went over to his wife and handed her the camera. "Come on, honey, take a picture of us." Robot-like, she followed his instructions.

"Okay, now you sit on her and I'll take a picture," he said.

"No, Michael. No. Please don't." Terror seized her. She turned to flee, but her movements were sluggish and slow because of the mud and water that suctioned her feet into the ground.

Michael reached for her and pulled her by the arm, laughing at her. "Don't be silly. Come on. You'll probably be the first woman to have her picture taken with a freshly killed moose," he exclaimed. He took the camera from her.

"No! No!" she screamed, as he tugged at her sweater, and the others laughed, enjoying the scene. Marlena pulled her thoughts together quickly. How could she convince Michael to leave her alone and let her go back to the truck.

"Please let go, Michael. I don't want to go over there. I'll get blood on my boots and jeans. Someone might stop me and question me. Besides, I have to get back to the truck and drive out. Someone might have spotted it already." Her mind sought excuses. She offered them all up to her husband, but he just laughed.

"Don't worry, honey. It'll only take a second. Besides, it's too foggy for anyone to see the truck."

"So why did you make me drive in?" she protested.

"Oh, come on. Be reasonable, will you? Even if someone sees the truck, no one's going to get excited about a truck that stops for a couple of minutes." With that, Michael drew her closer to the dead animal.

Marlena stumbled and fell on the carcass. Nick and Jim roared with delight. Michael let go of her and playfully ordered her to stay put. "Hold it. That's perfect. Don't move." He snapped a picture.

Marlena was horrified. She told her body to get up but it wouldn't obey. She could feel the huge lump of flesh beneath her. Her hands had instinctively gripped the coarse hairs. She could not let go. "Oh God, help me, help me. Please God, help," she pleaded hysterically.

"Okay, okay, stop shouting. Someone might hear you." Michael went over and lifted her from the carcass. Once up, she tried to flee, but the twigs and branches and the soggy earth impeded her retreat. A few moments before, these same obstacles had unsuccessfully attempted to prevent her from getting to this spot; now they were imprisoning her, holding her there, at the scene of the crime.

When she finally reached the pick-up, she heard Michael shout after her. "Don't forget – half an hour. Meet us at the gravel road." Nick's devilish roar echoed in her ears.

Marlena drove home as fast as the terrain allowed. But even the road had conspired against her. The rain had filled the ruts and the faster she went, the worse it was. Her head crashed to the roof of the truck's cabin each time she bumped over a hole. Her hands could barely control the steering wheel. She veered to the right trying to evade a trench-like depression that had formed where the gravel had slackened and found herself entangled in the bushes. She backed out, then accelerated and drove on.

At home, she ripped off her wet and bloody clothes. She washed and scrubbed her body. Like Lady Macbeth, she wondered if she would ever wash herself clean. She spit out her saliva continuously. She couldn't swallow it.

Marlena didn't go back. The men had to walk out. Nick was furious. Jim was disappointed. They glared at her in disgust. "I told you we shouldn't have counted on her," Nick said reproachfully. Michael apologized to them for his wife's foolishness.

"You and your bright ideas." Nick snarled at Jim.

Nick and Jim went home. At midnight they'd all go back in to bring the moose out.

"Why didn't you come back in for us?"

"I don't know."

"I thought you'd enjoy seeing a real live moose."

"It was dead."

"You know what I mean."

Michael went over to his wife and tentatively put his arms around her, as if testing the terrain before he lightly kissed her on the cheek. "Come on, honey. Don't spoil it," he said. He let her go and his mind returned to the hunt. "Boy, when I saw her there, in front of us, staring in our direction, I was scared, really scared."

"What happened to the other one?" Marlena asked.

"I don't know. Never did find her."

"What's going to happen to her?" Marlena was alarmed by her husband's complacency.

"She's no good to us any more anyway, even if we did find her."

"Why not?"

"She's probably blown up by now."

"Blown up? What do you mean?"

"They fill up with air and blow up, like a balloon . . . you know."

In her mind, Marlena saw a dead moose with a large, taut belly and, next to the cow, a little calf pined away. And now there was a second orphan. Two orphans in one day.

"What will happen to the little calf?"

"Oh, don't worry. It'll be okay. They can take care of themselves."

Marlena was confused. She couldn't understand. This one would be "okay"; it could take care of itself. What made it any different from the little calf Michael had spotted yesterday when he had been out there all alone? That calf had looked helpless to him.

At midnight, they were all set to go in for the moose. Marlena couldn't sleep.

They were home at three, covered with blood and mud. They looked like walking corpses. Some of the blood had caked on Michael's face and in his blond hair. Nick's red shirt just looked wet. They laughed when they saw themselves in the light. Nick said he was the smartest of the three because he had worn red.

They took off their boots and brownish muck splattered onto the floor. They asked for a pail of water to soak their socks. When they dropped them in, blood swirled through the icy water, and soon all of it was a cloudy maroon color. They stripped to their underwear. Marlena gave them clean, dry clothes. She picked up the bloody ones and hauled them into the bathtub. A little stream of blood trickled to the floor as she walked down the hall. When she dropped them in, the weight of the clothes made the blood splatter the bathroom walls. She turned on the tap. Then she got sick. They heard her retching.

"Women. They're all the same. No stomach," she heard Nick say. Michael was slightly embarrassed at his wife's behavior. She went to bed but she couldn't shut her eyes. If she did, the moose with the big belly appeared and she saw the men with blood all over them. She laid there in the dark and listened to them.

She heard how they had butchered the moose. It had still been warm when they stuck the knife into her. Off with the head. They slit it vertically along the belly, then eviscerated her. They took out the heart and liver. They threw the rest of the entrails into the bog. Then they quartered her.

Each man had hauled up a quarter. Michael had a hind. They had hauled the slabs of meat onto their shoulders and, with Jim leading the way, flashlight in hand, they had walked out in single file. No wonder they were exhausted.

Marlena's heart raced when she heard how Michael had slipped and gone into the bog. The weight of the hind quarter had made him sink into the spongy earth almost to the waist. Had he had been alone, he would never have gotten out alive, they said, taking credit for saving him. Had he been alone, she thought, perhaps none of this would have happened.

When three of the quarters were safely in the truck, they had all gone back to collect the remaining one. Then they had sped home.

The head was still out there in the woods. Marlena knew what it looked like. What if she, or someone else, came across it? Wide opened eyes staring ahead. That long snout. She envisioned the bodiless creature whose blood was in her house.

Early next morning, Michael scampered out to the truck like a child anxious to play. He called to Marlena. "Come on, honey. Come and look."

"No, Michael. I'd rather not."

"Don't be silly. Come on out. It won't frighten you anymore. It's cut into quarters now. Doesn't look the same."

She went. That strange force dragged her out, just as it had the day before. What did this creature she had fallen on look like now?

It was well covered with a sheet of plywood so dogs couldn't get at it. Even without the plywood it would have been safe since the truck had a makeshift cap on the back with a hinged door for access. They had been too exhausted to drag in the quarters the night before. It was cold outside. They had decided to leave the moose there until they could get at it to cut it up and package it.

Michael swung open the door and began to lift the plywood and Marlena saw the hoof and part of the leg.

"Stop, Michael. I don't want to look anymore."

"You women. So squeamish. You're going to help us freeze the meat, you know."

"No, not me."

Michael laughed at his wife and told her they had enough meat to last all winter. It was just as good as any of the steaks she bought at the store. She ate them, didn't she?

She didn't feel sorry for the juicy pieces of meat that sizzled on the barbecue many a night, did she?

"You cut through the belly and it was still warm, Michael. I heard you say so," she protested.

"Is that what's bothering you? Look, honey, it was dead. Sure it was warm because it hadn't been dead long. Now stop all this nonsense. You're a meat eater, just like the rest of us."

"I know, Michael, but this is different."

"No, it isn't. It's not different."

"Yes, it is. You hunted this one down. You went out there to get her. You didn't have to. You wanted to."

Who was she kidding? Michael was right. She was just drawing the curtain on the truth. She too ate meat. She checked her thoughts. How dare she accuse Michael of a primitive madness. How dare she blame Nick and Jim. Could it be that we all bend and twist and stretch ourselves to accommodate the ones we love only to snap back given the chance?

They came back that evening, their wives dutifully trailing behind them and the children jostling merrily. The women and Marlena were supposed to package the meat into plastic bags, label the cuts, and divide everything into three portions. Each family would get an equal share, even though it was Nick who had actually killed the moose.

Nick and Jim's kids went downstairs to gape at the quarters hanging from thick ropes tossed over the rafters. The children slapped the quarters, twirling them round and round in one direction, then they would wait for the pieces to stop and make them go the other way.

They grabbed on to the ropes, wrapped their legs around the meat and pushed themselves back and forth as if they were swings. The mothers reprimanded them. Marlena was mortified. The cat licked the dripping blood. The dog barked at the four monsters that dangled before him.

Marlena didn't want to freeze it yet. It hadn't drained properly. Besides, it was supposed to hang for a few days before being packaged. They hadn't given the sinews enough time to break up. It would be tough meat. Those were the reasons she gave for not wanting to help.

They told her they had no choice. It was much too warm in the basement to let it hang. Maggots would form and it would go bad. Then they would have to cut out the rotten parts and lose a lot of good meat. They couldn't risk hanging it in anyone's garage and they certainly couldn't bring it to a public freezer. They were poachers.

And so she straggled towards the tables they had set up for the job. Jim started to skin it. Michael helped. Nick looked on. He had actually brought it down, so he could sit back and let the others do most of the work now. They were jubilant. What a lark. Smiles on their contented faces. They were enjoying every minute. In the excitement, the men had forgotten their former anger towards Marlena.

They rehashed the events of the kill. They told their wives how Marlena had fallen on the moose. Everyone thought it was hilarious. They couldn't wait to see how the pictures turned out. She couldn't wait either. She wanted to tear them up and burn the evidence that she too had been an accomplice in this conspiracy against life.

Nick picked up the heart and showed it to Marlena. He told her she should stuff it and bake it in the oven. It was delicious that way.

Then he picked up the liver. Because of its texture and size, he needed both hands to do that. He looked at it with such pride. The quivering mass jiggled like jelly.

"We'll eat this later," he said. "Liver should be eaten

fresh." He turned to Marlena. "Didn't I promise you we'd get a moose? Look at this. Just look at this! Look at the size of it. It's beautiful! I almost want to eat it raw."

The others laughed at his suggestion.

"I wouldn't put it past you, you cannibal," Michael said. He turned to the women and told them how Nick had actually drunk some of the blood out there in the woods. "The man's primitive," he said, clearly applauding his friend's virility. The women didn't believe it; they said Michael had to be exaggerating.

Nick verified Michael's account. He swore he had drunk the blood. The women giggled and accepted Nick's bravado as one would accept a child's account of a superhuman feat.

Nick was insulted by the insinuation. To prove his point, he suddenly tore into the liver looking like the wild dogs Marlena had seen on television documentaries. He bit off a chunk of the blubbery organ saying: "Ah . . . ooh! It's super . . . delicious!"

Blood dripped through his fingers. It looked as if he had cut his hands. Blood oozed from the sides of his mouth. He bared his teeth to Marlena, clenching the chunk of liver between them. Blood outlined each tooth.

Everyone roared with laughter. The children thought it was hilarious.

"Look," his son said, "Daddy looks like a monster."

Then Nick went over to Marlena. He shoved the liver he was cradling in his bloody hands up to her face. "Come on!" he said. "Have a bite."

Michael was laughing too. Marlena saw him. Just before she got sick, just before her mind went into oblivion, she saw her husband's laughing face.

When she regained consciousness, she found herself in bed. The house was quiet. Michael was sitting at her side.

"It's okay, Marlena. They're gone," he assured her.

"Have they finished?" she asked.

"Yes."

"The basement, is it . . . ?"

"It's okay. I cleaned up. I gave Nick and Jim our share. I didn't keep any. I didn't put any in the freezer."

He looked deep into his wife's eyes as he told her this. He saw that same look on her face, the look she had had the other day when he'd come home and told her he hadn't been able to kill the moose.

"They've found the missing woman," my husband, Michael, mumbled from behind the newspaper.

"Oh?" I said, lowering the section I was reading. "Is she . . . ?" I hesitated.

"Dead," said Michael, finishing the sentence for me. "A jogger found the nearly decomposed body. That's what usually happens in these cases. Joggers, hunters, you know. The police have put two and two together: the missing woman, the body, dental records. They've come up with a Jo Menadra. They've even got a picture."

"Can I see?" I ask stretching my arm out for the paper, thinking, I must be sick to even want to look at it.

The name, Jo Menadra, had meant nothing, but the photo jolted me. I peered at it closely, disbelieving.

"I know this woman," I told Michael. "This is Giuseppina, you remember, that girl who was in the hospital with me when Johnny was born. The one who conned me into being her son's Godmother. Look closely," I stammered. "Remember? Her son was born the same day as Johnny."

I looked at the picture again. In it, Giuseppina wore that same red dress she'd donned when she left the hospital. And that same gold chain with the gaudy pendant of the Virgin Mary hung from her neck. I fought back an eerie sensation that made my flesh prickle.

A niggling feeling pushed me towards the phone. I told myself I should call Giuseppina's husband and offer my condolences, but it couldn't be the same man she'd been married to when I knew her. The name was different. I told myself I should at least call the son. Moses was his name. Such a strange name for a boy. But what would I say? I had made myself scarce for years.

She'd been a tiny little thing. Looked about twelve or thirteen. But she couldn't have been. After all, she was pregnant. And she didn't look the promiscuous type with that statue of the Blessed Virgin on her bedside table and that gold chain with the unusual pendant.

It had been the hottest day of the summer, even hotter than the five preceding ones which had been scorchers. Perhaps the heat had triggered my own discomfort, sending me to emergency that same day. I too was pregnant. Seven months and carrying my first child at the ripe age of thirty-three, I wasn't about to take any chances.

The hospital room was stifling and Giuseppina's continuous sobbing made it unbearable. With all the deep breaths she took between sobs, Giuseppina seemed to be sucking the air out of the room. I had opened the window because of the heat, but also to invite the street sounds in to drown out the continuous whining. The young girl was like a puppy, inconsolable, and pitiful.

Whenever a nurse came in, maneuvering blood pressure stands, charts, and thermometers, Giuseppina whimpered and whined even louder. She was pathetic.

I hadn't wanted to get to know her but circumstances dictated: our close proximity, boredom, our mutual worries, preoccupation for our unborn babies. Even I wasn't immune to the spell certain places and situations have on people: hospitals, airplanes, buses, trains; they tend to temporarily bind together in friendship the most unlikely candidates.

When Giuseppina heard the doctor's verdict on my condition – low blood pressure due to the fetal position and nothing more serious – she turned large, red-rimmed doe eyes towards me and attempted a smile. "I heard," she sniffled. "I'm glad *you're* going to be okay."

I felt obliged to be polite at this point and asked, "Why are you in?"

The flood gates opened and Giuseppina revealed all. Or so I thought at the time.

I had incorrectly suspected she was an unwed mother, the wedding band a cheap imitation to ward off snickers. There had been no sign of Rodolfo, the husband who was supposedly out of town on business. I didn't believe any of it, but was forced to change my malicious thoughts when Rodolfo showed up one night.

It was after visiting hours. Giuseppina and I were getting ready for bed when he walked in like an illicit dream. Giuseppina let out an excited wail.

He was a stunning specimen. Beautiful from the tips of his blue-black hair to his polished shoes. Piercing blue eyes, sensuous lips, and a neck any chain would have counted itself fortunate to adorn.

Rodolfo solemnly took Giuseppina's face into his beautiful hands and stared deeply into her eyes as if he were hypnotizing her. Trance-like, she smiled as tears flooded her face. He dropped one hand and slipped it beneath Giuseppina's blankets. The covers undulated as Rodolfo's hand traced her belly. Giuseppina closed her eyes in ecstasy.

When he left, her agitation was so great the sleeping pills had no effect on her. I couldn't sleep either. Rodolfo seemed to have left a powerful spirit in the room along with the scent of his cologne.

"Isn't he something?" Giuseppina whispered to me.

"That's an understatement," I admitted thinking about my own husband. Not that mine resembled the hunchback of Notre Dame, but he was a far cry from this assembly of perfection.

The story was that Rodolfo had been married before and had fathered children. Giuseppina's family, devout Italian Roman Catholics, objected to their daughter's involvement with this man. They vowed to disown Giuseppina if she persisted in this odious relationship and made good on their threat when she'd married him. Now she was pregnant with his child.

She'd attempted to break her family's silence, telling them she was carrying their grandchild. But this bit of news only exacerbated her situation. She told me, through a steady stream of tears, they had called her *"putana,"* a whore, and *"maledetta,"* a woman cursed. Ominous words she should have heeded.

Hearing this, my heart went out to her. It all seemed so old-fashioned and unfair, and I took the bait and lamented her predicament with her. When she begged me to be her son's Godmother, I couldn't refuse.

This had all happened long ago. Eighteen years almost to the day, to be precise. And now, here was Giuseppina, whom I hadn't seen in almost that many years, her photograph plastered on the front page of the local paper.

The next day, more gruesome details surfaced, details I didn't want to read but couldn't resist. I was as bad as those who stop and gawk at highway accidents.

She'd been decapitated, sexually assaulted, organs had been ripped from her body, her eyes gouged out like old

King Lear. I couldn't read on. I held the article out for Michael, who then seized it from me.

"Looks like your dead friend, Jo, alias Giuseppina, led quite a life," he said. "Seems that Rodolfo fellow was a bit loony. Thought he was Moses."

"Moses? That's what Giuseppina called her son. That's his name," I told my husband in disbelief.

He must not have heard me, because he just went on with more horrifying details about Rodolfo. "Had a harem, kept half a dozen women pregnant at all times. Wow, and look at this," he said with a snicker. "His women had contests to see who had the most orgasms." Michael went silent as his eyes widened.

"What? Tell me."

"This is sick," he said tossing the paper to the floor, as if he had suddenly discovered it was contaminated by a deadly virus. "I don't know how they can even print this shit."

I gathered the paper off the floor and read. Not only did Rodolfo think he was Moses, he also thought he was a healer. He "operated" on women if they complained of a malady, chopping off an arm from one victim who claimed she had stiff fingers . . . Oh, it was too gruesome to read. He'd had communes all over the place, from B.C. to the east coast. Recently, he'd moved back to this part of the country, the faithful flock following like sheep. He was a cult figure.

Evidence of his debauchery surfaced from the incredible tales being told by the woman who had lost her arm. She had somehow survived the ordeal and managed to escape. Unfortunately, when she led the police to the camp site, Rodolfo was gone.

All night I couldn't get Giuseppina out of my mind. I tossed and turned, thinking, who could have done this to her? Was it really Rodolfo? Or could it have been her son? Her sister? Who? For I knew something about Giuseppina I had never told anyone, not even Michael. She had lied to me. Or, at the very least, she had not told me the whole truth. Years after I met Giuseppina I was introduced to her older sister, Monica. It was she who told me Rodolfo had been *her* husband. Giuseppina had coveted him and taken her brother-in-law. The little martyr had pulled the wool over my eyes. I felt deceived, betrayed, used.

That night, I dreamed of Giuseppina. Ghastly scenes played in my subconscious mind. I must have screamed, because I awoke to find Michael hovering over me. "Marlena," he called. "It's okay. Just a nightmare." I told him then how Giuseppina had deceived me.

Her funeral was the next day, which also happened to be my son and her son's birthday. A coincidence? Even the weather seemed programmed for the upcoming events. It was an unbearably hot and muggy day, reminiscent of that summer long ago. Nothing was going to keep me from attending. Not the heat, not my husband who warned me to keep my distance from these psychos, not even my own boy's party later that day.

"Don't be a sucker," Michael warned when he saw me donning black.

"I'm going," I insisted. "Curiosity is killing me. I'll be back in time," I promised.

"Please don't," he begged. "You don't owe her anything – especially after what you told me last night."

Undaunted, I left.

I hoped Rodolfo would show up. Instead, I found the funeral parlor nearly empty. An old man sat by the closed casket and an even older woman sat next to him. Neither was crying.

An anorexic looking youth walked in, and I glanced at him, wondering if it could be Moses, Giuseppina's son. The boy wore a T-shirt and tight jeans and a jean jacket. He had a full head of black hair, long and wavy, which seemed to slap his face as he walked. It looked like a girls' head, but the lanky body gave him away.

He and the old man nodded to each other, nothing more. I searched for traces of Rodolfo in the boy but could find few. I braced myself, deciding to offer him my condolences. When I saw the piercing blue eyes, I knew it was Moses.

"I knew your mother," I told him.

He looked at me with those glossy eyes, question marks written all over them. He didn't bother to push aside the hair hiding part of his face.

"You're Moses, aren't you? Your mother and I were in the hospital together when you and my son were born. Eighteen years ago today." I couldn't bear to tell him I was also his Godmother. I hoped he didn't know.

Still no reaction. He just looked away like a blind man hearing voices, trying to make out where they were coming from. When he turned to leave, like a moth drawn to a flame, I did the same. It was as if he had invited me to do so.

If Moses knew I was following him, he showed no evidence of it. Perhaps he was drugged, because he seemed completely oblivious to me. He drove an old jeep, making it easy to tail him. He left the city and headed into the country. It was hotter now, nearly noon. The sun beat down from its zenith. I turned the air conditioner up full blast and pointed the vents towards my perspiring face.

He veered off the main highway and onto a gravel road. Dust flew into the air, obliterating my view of the jeep, but, of course, the powdery cloud I trailed confirmed Moses was still ahead.

He drove to a wooded area, then turned into a bumpy, rutted track. The heat had dehydrated the earth, compacting it to an almost concrete hardness.

I drove ahead to avoid being obvious, parked me car, then walked back. I followed the trail until I came to a clearing. I saw three low tents the same dark green as the foliage in the trees. Debris and garbage were scattered all around the camp. The stench assaulted my nostrils.

A snapping sound behind me sent me spinning. As I turned, a large bearded figure suddenly threw himself upon me, pinning me to the ground. His long hair fell wildly to his shoulders. I struggled in vain, frantically squirming and twisting until his hands stilled me, pressing my shoulders to the hard earth. Gasping for breath, I looked up into my assailant's eyes. It was Rodolfo. He had the look of a demented maniac. He pulled me to my feet and led me to one of the tents. Inside, he threw me to the floor in front of a makeshift altar and told me to repent. "Kneel," he commanded. "Kneel at the altar of Moses and repent."

Trembling, I dropped to my knees.

"Prepare thyself," he barked. When he dashed from the tent, I looked for an escape route. An altar stood in one corner: two cement blocks with a wood plank across them. Several other blocks stood on their ends like small stands. On these he had meticulously assembled a collection of miniature figures: tiny elves, miniature dolls, diminutive busts, and an assortment of peculiar paraphernalia.

Before I could do anything, I heard a clanging and a rush of feet. I nervously peered out to witness a rabble of women and children swarming towards me. Two of the older women dashed in and dragged me out, ripping and tearing off my clothes. I fought like a trapped animal, but they held me in an iron grip.

"You need to be purified," they chanted. "He will then sow the seed of Moses into you."

Another impromptu altar had been set up in the clearing. I was nearly delirious with fear as the two women threw me onto this low platform. The rough wood tore my flesh. Was I to become a sacrificial offering?

Fear stole my voice, my mouth opened and shut like a dying fish. I looked out, my eyes pleading for assistance. My silent plea was answered by demented stares. As I scanned the zombie-like crowd, I saw visions of Giuseppina. So many faces looked like hers.

Through my tears, islands of red stood out in relief. All the women and children wore a red talisman: a headband, a kerchief, a vest.

Rodolfo burst from his tent wearing a red cape and a crown of plaited twigs. The women and children knelt and bowed in adoration. Or was it fear?

As Rodolfo began to straddle the altar and me, the gold chain with the pendant of the Madonna slipped from his tunic and swung like a pendulum of doom above my face. It was Giuseppina's chain.

Suddenly, a deafening blast echoed through the forest. Rodolfo sprawled urgently and unexpectedly upon me, his weight crushing and suffocating me. Panting like an exhausted dog, I strained to push him off.

What? Blood? My God, was he dead? I felt the warmth of his blood on my body. I lay back unflinching, his dead weight strangulating me.

The women and children screamed and ran in all directions like frightened chickens. From under the oppressing hulk, I looked up to see Moses, the son, a rifle raised to his cheek. I lay paralyzed. If he fired again, he might kill me too.

Numbed, he drew himself near me, as my heart pumped furiously against my chest. With his boot, Moses kicked the corpse from me. My arms instinctively attempted to cover my nakedness. Moses stripped the red cape from the dead man and handed it to me. I wiped the blood from my flesh and covered my bare body.

"Come," he said. "You have to get out of here."

"How did you know he was here?" I asked breathlessly. "Is this where you've been living all this time?"

"No," Moses whispered. "But I remembered."

"Remembered?"

"From when I was young."

So Rodolfo had been here before. This was probably where he had kept poor Giuseppina. This was probably where he had taken her when little Moses was born. Oh, God, I thought, what else can this poor boy remember?

"Hurry," Moses called. "The police will be here soon."

"The police?"

"I called. Told them there'd been a shooting."

He led me to my car and helped me in. "Hurry," he said urgently. "Go."

"What about you?" I asked.

"Go." he insisted.

He slammed my car door shut and turned, retracing his steps.

"Don't go back there," I implored him. "Come with me."

He walked steadily towards the grisly scene, like a deaf man. I thought of my own son and my husband. I thought about poor Giuseppina. I turned the key in the ignition and looked back one final time. Moses had disappeared into the bush.

That was when I heard the gun go off again. Just one loud blast, and then there was silence.

FOR BETTER OR FOR WORSE

Dad is slouched in an off-white armchair next to his side of the bed. The chair has been temporarily draped in a spotless towel. All he has on is a pair of boxers, bleached a milky white. They match his skin. Mom is slathering a creamy white lotion across his scrawny shoulders. She hasn't noticed his flaccid penis dangling from the slit in the shorts. It looks like a skinny, shriveled up hot dog. He, of course, is oblivious to his exposed appendage.

Sachets of potpourri hang from doorknobs. An enormous dried flower arrangement, filled with masses of eucalyptus, sits on the dresser. The pungent scents waft through the air in tenuous currents, but they are no match for the medicinal smells infusing the room.

On the meticulously made bed covered in white eyelet lace, my father's clothes are laid out perfectly: a crispy white long-sleeved shirt, something he wears on a daily basis, even at home, because Mom says he can only have white clothing next to his delicate skin, precision pressed beige wool slacks, white cotton pyjama bottoms to go over the boxers and under the slacks, an olive green cashmere sweater, socks of no ordinary cotton but of *filo di scotzia* imported from Italy, the only concession to color allowed to come in contact with his sensitive dermis, and a tan leather belt to complete the ensemble. The Duke of Windsor. That's the look she aims for.

I swallow the bile in my mouth and summon all the tact

I can muster. "Almost ready?" I call from the doorway, sounding perky.

"Just the legs left," my mother assures me in an equally perky tone. As an aside she whispers audibly, "They're the worse."

I want to tell her, Dad isn't deaf yet, but he interjects before I have a chance.

"Oh shut up, woman," he says sharply. "This is all her idea," he snaps. "She's nuts. A fanatic."

Mom purses her lips. "Oh sure. I'm nuts. He sheds so much my carpets are white with scale."

"So what."

"So what? I have to shake out the sheets every day, that's what," she complains turning to me. "When I flick them into the air, it looks like a blizzard outside."

"Women. Crazy women. Everything has to be neat and clean and perfect. God damn it. Dirt is healthy."

"This isn't dirt."

"Exactly," he exclaims straightening himself up as if he's just won a poker game.

"It's skin. It's scale."

"But it ain't dirt."

"Hey, you two," I intrude to referee. "I thought we were going shopping?"

Dad twists around and wrenches the lotion from my mother. "Right. Let's go. Enough of this nonsense."

"But, John . . . your legs . . . look at them. Those black socks'll be white as soon as you . . . "

"God damn it, woman, get white socks . . . Like all the other stuff."

Mom retreats. I can't help thinking, would the Duke of Windsor have worn white socks?

Dad stands. His penis slips back into his boxers. His skinny scrawny legs are almost translucent. The blue veins seem much too close to the surface. The scales are like fish scales, all over his legs. Whenever I scrape fish I think of my Dad. He is shedding, crumbling. As far as my mother is concerned, all the flaky, scaly stuff is clogging up the house. Like the gritty mess that settles at the base of water taps, in humidifier reservoirs or tea pots. All that annoying lime-like residue that always needs to be taken care of, cleaned, scrubbed off vigorously, brushed, or soaked away with some chemical or other. My father is depositing residue all over the house, over his Duke of Windsor clothes, his bed linen, the furniture. He is a heap of disintegrating flesh.

My mother has pursed her lips so tightly they look anal. The tiny crows feet converge at the little puckered lips. Her eyes dart about the room, as if looking for something to support her. Something she can grab on to.

Seeing all his clothes are still on the bed, she goes over and stares down at each piece: the shirt, the pants, the sweater, the socks, the belt. She looks weary and yet I can still detect a determined spark in her. For the moment, she is not going to cause a scene. She unfurls her pursed lips and stretches them into a semi-smile for me. "He needs to get out more," she tells me. "Being cooped up in here all day is making him edgy."

Dad sneezes forcefully, disrupting the air currents in the room. "Being cooped up in here is killing me," he snorts wiping his nose on a handkerchief mother proffers. "It's like being in a funeral home."

"Chronic sinusitis," she confides to me, as if this is a new diagnosis I know nothing about.

"Maybe you should get rid of all the dried flowers," I suggest tactfully. "They can't be doing him any good."

"Nonsense," mother insists. "That nice doctor specialist your husband sent us to said your father's problems are all due to erectile tissue in his sinuses."

"What?" I blurt, aghast at her choice of words.

My father snickers. "Son of a bitch. Here we go again with the erectile tissue."

My father has always peppered his speech with titillating vocabulary but this is something new for my mother. He sometimes finds her new propensity for things sexual humorous, but not when he is the target.

She continues undaunted. "That doctor said the tissue swells when your father's in a prone position . . . 'Prostrate' was the word he used, but he said it has nothing to do with the prostate," she clarifies. "I asked," She clarifies further. "When he lies down, it plugs up his nose and he can't breathe. Nothing to do with my flower arrangements at all."

"Son of a bitch," Dad swears. "Listen to the mouth on her. Why didn't you talk like that when you were younger?" he yells, his hands undulating over his head. "Are you going to tell her how you informed the doctor the erectile tissue was in the wrong place?"

I pick up the socks. "Here, Dad. Now hurry up and get dressed."

They both detest these new fangled warehouse shopping stores, but that is where they want to go today.

The warehouse is a gigantic building with thousands of square feet of grey concrete blocks, grey concrete floors, grey steel support beams, grey shopping carts. A decorator's hell. Mom and Dad fit right in. They too look washed out and as drab as the building: hair, skin, eyes. Color has been bleached out of them; time has faded them the way sun fades fabric.

Dad takes a cart. It is so huge it looks like he's wheeling around a steel hospital bed with the sides up.

The complaints begin like drizzle, but I know it will soon be pouring. Where is my protective umbrella? My vinyl rain-coat. Be sweet and charming and understanding, I tell my-self. That's your best defense. Your best protection. Be pliable and resilient, not firm and tough.

"Did you two forget I've had a hip replacement?" he grum-bles. "How the hell do you expect me to get around this football field."

"John," Mother placates. "Why don't you go sit over there." She points to a drab eating area where more grey in the form of tables and chairs and umbrellas await shoppers, but this cordoned-off island of warehouse hospitality, even with its aroma of hot coffee, hot dogs and hamburgers, does not attract my father.

"Want to get rid of me, don't you? So you can spend a fortune in this Disneyland of groceries."

"Well, then, just come along slowly. We'll go slowly, won't we?" she assures him looking up at me with her automatic pleading smile which quickly reverts to her anal pucker.

"Of course. There's no rush." I play the game, strangling the thoughts that want to find a voice. I know the rules. I dare not volley back my real feelings.

"What the hell is that stink?" Dad mutters as we pass one of the food displays.

"Fish sticks, Dad."

"It stinks, alright."

I had welcomed this temporary relief from the smells of concrete, cardboard, and chemicals.

Mother purses her lips clam-like now. Her eyes glance at the woman preparing the fish sticks and she shakes her head: her way of asking forgiveness for her husband's rudeness.

Mother stops by the chickens in the rotisserie, plump and golden, basting in their own juices as they rotate round and round on the spit. "Oh, they look lovely."

"Get one, Mom."

"How much are they?"

"What does it matter? You have to eat, don't you?"

She glances back to see where Dad is. Far enough away. "He doesn't like chicken," she whispers *sotto voce*.

"What does he like?" I blurt out.

"Now, now. No need to get hostile," she warns.

I pick up a packaged chicken and place it in the cart which we are now pushing since Dad abandoned it at the fish sticks.

When Dad becomes aware of the offence, his hands dive into the cart to pluck the chicken out, nearly dropping it. "That son of a bitch." He swears at the chicken. "Hotter than Hades."

"What are you doing, Dad?"

"What does it look like?"

"Mom wants it."

"I don't eat chicken. No teeth."

My blood boils. Outrage. "It's not for you, Dad. It's for

her." I take the package out of the case again and deposit it back into the cart.

He mutters obscenities and Mother reprimands me. "You shouldn't have done that," she says.

There are further battles over bananas (constipating for him, potassium for her), cucumbers (he can't digest them, she finds them refreshing), ice cream (with his teeth and gums they make him see stars, she wants to gain a little weight.)

Round one, I think. A draw so far?

"Why don't we take a break?" I suggest. "Have something to drink. My treat."

Dad commandeers the cart and leads us over to the depressing eating area with the umbrellas. I settle them in the way one settles in children and go for three coffees.

I stand in line for the coffee and take in deep breaths of warehouse air. I am glad to be out of my parents' range for a bit. Their presence stifles me. They are like a couple of annoying mosquitoes buzzing about the bedroom on a hot and humid summer night.

I look at the time and think of Michael who is home, snug in bed. I want to be with him. My parents will only grace the outside world with their presence during this time of the day. Before is "too early" and after is "too late." Besides, Michael needs his rest. He'll be up soon for the afternoon shift at the hospital.

Mother daintily sips her coffee. Dad slurps a mouthful, burning his tongue. "Son of a bitch," he swears.

"He's always doing something silly these days," Mom says. "This morning, for instance. Before you arrived. He vacuumed his balls."

"Jesus Christ, woman," Dad screeches. "Is nothing sacred?"

"I'm just trying to tell her how you're always doing something crazy these days."

"What are you two talking about?"

"He got the bright idea to get out the vacuum cleaner to clean all that scale from his pants. Didn't figure the thing would suck in his balls."

"Mother, are you talking about what I think you're talking about?'

Pursed lips again, a lowered chin, her tiny grey eyes as wide as she can get them making it quite clear we were talking testicles here.

"I heard him squeal like a pig being butchered."

"Jesus Christ." Dad slides his chair back forcefully, the unsteady table shakes and his Styrofoam cup of coffee splashes over his trousers. "God damn it. Now I've scalded them," he shouts.

I run for paper towels as curious shoppers pretend not to watch.

On our way home in the car, they are at each other. Dad on the attack with Mom managing to duck the punches and sometimes even delivering a jab below the belt. "Your groin is a mess anyway, John." Turning to me, the referee, she has to add, "You should see his groin area. That lotion your dear doctor husband sent hasn't done much. He's all red and raw-looking . . . "

"Woman, if you don't shut up . . . "

It was almost entertaining. My mother talking in sexually explicit terms. The woman who explained my first menstruation saying, "You can have a baby now, dear," as if at eleven it was time to trade in my doll.

I glance at my watch again. Almost two o'clock. Michael will be getting ready for work. Showering, no doubt. I picture his naked body. A twinge of desire flushes through me. But I can't make it home before he leaves.

That night I dream Michael is old and grey and scrawny, and his skin is pale and delicate and scaly. I awake with a start, sweating and gasping. My hand searches the night table for the clock. Eleven-thirty. Michael's shift will be over soon. I'll get up and make some camomile tea, get back into bed and wait for him.

There, headlights illuminate the bedroom window, I can hear the garage door going up, the car pulling in. My body tingles with anticipation.

He slides into bed naked. I snuggle up to him. He is already aroused.

"How was your shopping spree?" he asks.

"You're amazing," I say.

"Are you referring to my sexual prowess?"

"That too. But you ask about my shopping spree. God only knows what you've seen tonight."

"Nothing as tantalizing as you," he says. He is becoming more amorous. His sensitive doctor hands know what to do.

"Is this a physical?" I joke.

"You're so tense," he tells me, molding my body to his, trying to untie the knots.

"I was just having a bad dream. What does the doctor recommend?"

"I have an age-old stress buster. Been on the market for years and still doing brisk business."

"I saw my father's penis today."

"A frightening sight, I'm sure," he snickers. "Look what it's done to your mother."

"I'm not joking."

"A daughter should not see a father's penis. A wife, on the other hand . . . "

My father's image keeps getting in the way. The dream is still too fresh in my mind. Every part of Michael's body I touch brings an image of my father: a flaccid penis dangling from boxers, skinny scrawny shoulders, chicken legs, knobby knees and elbows, a conical Adam's apple bobbing up and down, thin, unsmiling lips. The robustness of Michael's body is in such sharp contrast.

Had Dad been like this once? I wonder. Had my mother waited with anticipation for him to slide into bed beside her? When she slathers his decrepit body with lotions, what does she see? What does she feel? Frail loose flesh or satiny softness? Bony projections or strong, muscle bound arms and legs?

Michael intercepts my thoughts. "Where is that arduous woman who was in my bed a few minutes ago?" he jokes.

These are frightening thoughts of the unknown, of a future I want no part of. But I have no crystal ball. For better or for worse. That was the vow taken. For better or for worse.

I stretch my arm and turn on the bedside lamp. Michael releases me. "Refusing to take your medicine, are you?"

"I want to look at you. Imprint your face into my memory chamber for future reference."

I bend over him and kiss him. This was the "for better" part. If "the worse" was programmed, so be it. I will retrieve these images, play them on my mind's screen. I will relive the good times.

THE T-SHIRT MAN

It was Saturday. The sun rose over the Caribbean and prepared itself for this week's group of migrants. The T-shirt man did the same.

He shuffled across his one room shack rubbing sleep from his eyes. Outside, calypso music stirred the air, dogs barked, chickens cackled. Later, in the heat of the day, they would all be silent.

The new arrivals would still be sleeping. They had come in on the late night flight, as usual.

The T-shirt man's wife was already sitting on her dilapidated doorstep looking out at other women sitting on their own versions of the same. He walked over and stood beside her for a moment. He too inspected the street, then turned and went back into his shack. From beneath the makeshift bed he dragged out his scarred and scratched suitcase. His wife glanced over her shoulder, then resumed her former lackadaisical position.

"You sell them T-shirt too cheap," she accused.

"Woman, don't start," he said. But he knew she was right.

"Too cheap. Worth twice what you asking."

He clenched his teeth and packed more shirts into the suitcase. He put one on, pulled on a pair of brown pants, and left. Perspiration beaded his forehead. It was hard to say which had put it there: the heat or the woman.

His wife watched him disappear down the street. She

watched his swiveling hips and his tight buttocks. The other women watched too.

He walked past the real town and into the make believe town. Some of the people from the real town worked in the make believe town. The girls and women cooked and cleaned for those who didn't; the boys and men carried luggage, watered plants, cut grass. The T-shirt man did not do these things.

This was why he did not stop in the make believe town. He sliced his way through and headed down to the beach. He went to where the breeze could lift the drudgery from his soul, evaporate the sweat that oozed continually through his skin, as if it was being replenished by a mysterious, subcutaneous reservoir.

There were morning customers and afternoon customers. A few were both. These were the ones who lavishly massaged lotion into each other's skins. These were the ones who would be there to greet the sun and bid it farewell, intent upon the task at hand: absorb the blistering rays. Out of the corner of his eye he could see them luxuriating in the sensuality of it all. The men, rubbing hard and deep, teasing and bringing forth giggles of pleasure whenever their heavy hands purposely reached beneath the tiny coverings. The women, lubricating with fingers that played a prelude.

The T-shirt man was used to this. In the beginning, when the tourists first started coming to the island, he used to wonder why anyone would sit in the sun. These people bared themselves and baked all day. They slithered into the water to cool their sweating bodies, then returned to the smooth, hot sand to begin the basting process anew. The islanders rarely went into the water. If they did, it was to fish or scout for clams, not to romp and frolic.

The young tourist girl slept in. She hadn't rested well. She blamed it on the room. It overlooked a street and the roadway had been teeming with activity most of the night. Music, loud and pulsating, singing, laughing, screeching tires.

But the sun was persistent. The sun demanded she waken. Not even the curtains could keep it out. Her closed eyelids knew it was there. They had become eggshells. The burning bulb of the sun forced them open.

Marlena peeled the curtains from the window and a giant mango tree stared back at her. Hibiscus hedge rimmed the hotel grounds and beyond she saw a lime tree so full of fruit it didn't seem real. Bananas, smaller than the ones she was used to, hung heavy from a large leaved tree. An enormous poinsettia made her distrust her eyes. Could she ever look at a potted Christmas plant again and not think of this?

She forgot about the heat and she forgot about the noise of the night before and she forgot all discomforts. She was enchanted.

The T-shirt man never had any trouble spotting the new arrivals with their pale, sickly looking skin. They were unsure of themselves, not knowing how to respond. They were still polite when they were white. The darker they got, the less they bought. They became more confident and told him to "go away" as soon as he encroached upon their patch of beach. It was strange how they could change in just a few days.

So he went for the whities, and left the others alone. They all went for the whities: those who sold trinkets and phony coral necklaces, those who sold imitation flowers and straw baskets. Everyone worked the whities, especially on a

Saturday morning when new arrivals were at their weakest and ready for the novelty.

The T-shirt man went up to the tourist girl sitting alone on the beach. He knelt beside her and opened his suitcase. "You like to buy?" he asked.

"Oh, how lovely!" she said when she saw the T-shirts.

"I show you, Missy. Best T-shirts you can buy." He handed her a shirt. It had a palm tree on it.

"Good Lord," she said. "This is nice. I mean, where do you get them? They're the nicest T-shirts I've ever seen."

"What I tell you?" he said.

"No, seriously. These are fine quality. How much?"

He told her the price and she looked up at him.

"Too much?" he asked.

"Too much? You must be kidding. You couldn't get these back home for twice that. I'll take a couple."

The T-shirt man was glad his wife was not there to hear the tourist girl.

The T-shirt man went back in the afternoon. She was there again. Under a palm, in its shade. Alone. When she saw him, she waved. He waved back. But he didn't go to her. He didn't try to sell her another T-shirt.

How unlike the others who pestered constantly, she thought to herself.

She watched him go up and down the beach, endlessly retracing his steps. She watched him go up to the tourists. Some bought; some didn't. Sometimes he smiled; sometimes he frowned and once in a while she thought she saw him search her out.

She noticed he wore the same brown pants rolled up to

just below the knee. He didn't want to get them wet. And he was always barefoot, his sandals slung over a shoulder. He looked impeccably clean wearing one of his snowy white T-shirts with the island motif stretched across his broad torso.

There was something about him. He possessed an illusive quality the other vendors did not have and she caught herself observing the T-shirt man hour after hour, day after day.

At night, he held her thoughts and invaded her dreams. In them, the T-shirt man and Michael became as one, indistinguishable. But when she woke, trembling and shuddering with passion and desire, she was always alone.

Day after day she waited for the man. He was becoming an obsession. She knew this.

What the tourist girl didn't know was that she too was becoming an obsession with him.

They observed each other from a distance. He watched her skin transform and he marveled at the warm bronze tones that gleamed from her figure. She seemed to be darkening magically. Perhaps she had a potion. He knew she was still white in those places where the sun had not been invited. He pictured her naked: the velvet whiteness of her secret skin beside the golden expanse of tan. He pictured the line across her abdomen and buttocks, the circle around her breasts. And he longed for his darkness to penetrate her whiteness.

She went out to her usual spot and waited for him this morning. Her eyes combed the distance until they came upon him. She knew his walk. His swaying hips, the muscular frame, his head held high, suitcase propped on one shoulder, sandals on the other. She waved him over.

"I want to get a couple more before I leave."

"Going soon?"

"Few more days."

Even as she said it she wondered why this had to be. What was there to go back to? An empty room and a cool bed. Michael had left; she had done the same, hoping distance and a change would soothe her aching heart. She hadn't expected anything like this.

He cast his glance over the sea as she fished into her straw bag for the money. He didn't want to look at her. She paid him and thanked him. As he closed his suitcase, he took out another T-shirt. "This one free. For you."

"Oh, no. I couldn't."

"Yes, yes. For you. No money."

"No, I just couldn't. It isn't right. I have nothing for you."

"Please take," he implored.

"I'll pay for it." And she went to her bag again for the money. But he cupped his brown hand over hers. The touch of his hand seared her desire. She looked up at him, her eyes aching to find a meaning for the emotions flooding her.

"No," he insisted. "It is free." He smiled nervously, then realized his hand still covered hers.

When he got home, his wife was sitting on the doorstep. She slid sideways so he could get by.

He took off his shirt and pants and fell limply upon the bed. His wife came in. She sauntered over to the suitcase and began counting the T-shirts, then checked the money in the pocket of his brown pants.

"Sell a few today, I see."

But when she finished counting the money, she noticed: "Somebody take your T-shirt?"

"What you talking about, woman?"

"One shirt missing."

"You crazy, woman."

"I know. I count. Everyday I count. You think I'm stupid?"

He pulled on his pants and went back into the street. There was no peace.

The young tourist girl decided to walk towards town. The real town. She had heard about it. People at the hotel and the other tourists had told her not to go.

"Are you crazy? Nobody goes there."

"They do. They live there."

"Sure, they do. But you can't go there. It stinks. It's filthy. Running sewers in the street. They live in makeshift shacks with no plumbing, no running water."

"Jesus! They *live* there! They eat and sleep there, and they're still alive. Surely I can walk there?"

"They're used to it. Don't be so naive."

They tried to talk sense into her, but she wouldn't listen. They gave up. What did they care. It was her life.

The T-shirt man got up and went to the door. It was Friday and he knew last week's group would be leaving tonight. No point going down to the beach. Waste of time. He just stood in the doorway. He didn't see her coming up the street. Not yet. Those who did stared: some curiously, some suspiciously, some cynically. Everything she had heard about the real town was true. Women swaying lazily, going nowhere.

Men leaning up against frail structures. Naked children, running and playing in the dust. Dogs lying in the shade, tongues dripping, bellies rising and falling in a race to keep cool. Music in the background. Laughter punctuating and piercing the muffled sounds of the town. All doors open, displaying the innards of the dwellings. Beds here and there, a crippled table and chairs that didn't match. A small black and white television set perched on an infirm end table. Plastic flowers, plastic fruit, holy pictures, crosses and calendars.

Coming up on her right, a sign, tacked in place by a single rusty nail, signaling a restaurant. Reclaimed wood and boards thrown together to create a shelter. Three wood tables all scratched and bruised. A few wood chairs, paint chipped, legs wobbling. Behind it, a stove and some blackened, dented utensils. The tourist girl wondered what the old lady cooked and who ate there.

Down the road, a butcher shop. The same construction as the rest. No refrigerator in sight. Meat hanging from giant hooks. A couple of goats dripping blood. Chickens hanging by their skinny legs. Those that had not yet taken their place on the hooks above, pecked the goat drippings on the dusty ground. Flies paraded around the carcasses.

A violent stench filled the air. A putrid smell of decay. Here, vibrant flowers did not scent the air. Here, there were no ornamental plantings to trim, no grass to cut, no potted plants to water.

And then she saw him in the doorway: same brown pants, shirtless. His broad shoulders visible to her for the first time. He was deftly rolling a cigarette. There was a woman beside him. The cigarette must have been for her. He moistened the paper with his tongue, pressed the flimsy sheet together, and handed it to the woman.

The young tourist girl didn't want him to see her. She didn't want him to know she had witnessed him and his woman in their intimacy. It was too late. Their eyes met. He threw down his own cigarette and went into the shelter of his shack. His shame rang out. All he could do was hide.

She yearned to follow. She yearned to tell him he need not be ashamed. It was she who should be ashamed. Ashamed of her whiteness and all the luck it had brought her. Ashamed of her power to come and usurp him and his island. The T-shirt man had nothing to be ashamed of. He sold the finest T-shirts she had ever seen. She was wearing one now, proudly. The one he had given her.

From inside the tiny shack, the T-shirt man looked out between the slats. He watched the tourist girl walk up the road. In his frenzy to get out of view, he hadn't noticed her wearing his T-shirt. Now, from the privacy of his quarters, he saw.

A smile lightened his face. And he went down on his bed and dreamed of her whiteness and when he awoke it was Saturday and the sun rose over the Caribbean and prepared itself for this week's group of migrants. The T-shirt man did the same.

AGMV Marquis

MEMBER OF SCABRINI MEDIA

Quebec, Canada
2001